I0715972

Left in Philadelphia

Spencer Virden

Left in Philadelphia
First Edition 2024

By Spencer Virden
Copyright © 2024 Spencer Virden

Edited by Reprospace, LLC
Cover Design by Spencer Virden

ISBN 13: 978-1-952685-74-3

Kitsap Publishing
Poulsbo, WA • USA

REFLECTIONS

Spencer Virden's writing style can be compared to modernist and existentialist writers who emphasize introspection, the exploration of the human psyche, and finding meaning (or lack thereof) in the ordinary aspects of life. It has a reflective, somewhat melancholic tone that captures the complexities of human relationships and the search for purpose in a way that is very characteristic of Woolf, Joyce, and Camus.

The writing style of *"Left in Philadelphia"* shares similarities with several notable authors, particularly those who explore the mundane details of daily life and the inner workings of their characters' minds. Here are a few authors to whom Spencer Virden's style could be compared:

Virginia Woolf: The introspective, stream-of-consciousness style, especially Eli's internal monologues and reflections, resembles the work of Virginia Woolf. Woolf's novels, such as Mrs. Dalloway and To the Lighthouse, delve deeply into the thoughts and perceptions of the characters, often blurring the line between inner dialogue and external reality, much like Eli's reflections throughout the narrative.

James Joyce: The detailed internal exploration of the protagonist, the narrative's non-linear flow, and the emphasis on seemingly mundane events recall the style of James Joyce, particularly Ulysses. Joyce's work often captures the ordinary with extraordinary attention to internal thought processes, which is evident in Eli's narrative as he contemplates his life's direction and relationships.

J.D. Salinger: The introspective voice of Eli, with a slightly cynical edge and a keen sense of detachment, can also be reminiscent of J.D. Salinger's work, particularly The Catcher in the Rye. The protagonist's disillusionment and introspective nature parallel Holden Caulfield's reflections on his life and relationships.

Albert Camus: The existential undertones and themes questioning the meaning of life evoke Albert Camus, particularly The Stranger. Eli's musings about the mundanity of existence and his sense of detachment from life's conventional milestones are akin to Camus' focus on the absurdity and randomness of life.

Karl Ove Knausgård: The style also has elements that are similar to the autobiographical introspection found in Karl Ove Knausgård's My Struggle series. The narrative's focus on detailing everyday events while diving into the protagonist's psyche is similar to Knausgård's detailed and often painfully honest portrayal of ordinary life.

"I want to write a novel about silence. The things people don't say."

— Virginia Woolf

For those who
find beauty in quiet moments and
meaning in life's smallest details.

FOREWORD

In *Left in Philadelphia*, Spencer Virden has crafted a quiet yet powerful narrative, one that subtly touches on the complexities of the human condition. At its heart is Eli Greene, a man who navigates life with a deep sense of introspection, often retreating into the safety of his own thoughts. His journey is not one filled with grand adventures or dramatic moments, but rather with the quiet, sometimes painful reflections of a man coming to terms with his emotions and place in the world.

Through Eli's lens, we glimpse the subtle struggles of those who find themselves at odds with the world around them. His reluctance to fully engage with relationships, his acceptance of life's mundanity, and his ongoing questioning of love, purpose, and control suggest a deeply personal experience that resonates with many. It is a reflection of the challenges faced by individuals who quietly grapple with feelings of isolation, avoidance, or emotional detachment—whether they recognize it or not.

This story is not explicitly about mental health, yet it invites us to consider the ways in which we cope with life's uncertainties and hardships. Eli's journey reminds us that each of us carries our own quiet battles, and that understanding, acceptance, and empathy are essential as we move through the complexities of human experience.

As you read *Left in Philadelphia*, we hope you'll take a moment to reflect on the ways in which the small, often overlooked details of our lives can reveal the depth of our inner worlds. For Eli, it's these moments that ultimately shape his path, and perhaps, in his story, you may find pieces of your own.

INTRODUCTION

Let me speak candidly: what you are about to read is wholly composed of instances made from fiction. The characters, the situations, and the places are all fiction. That is what is so fascinating, or deceiving, about the genre; something that may seem so authentic is most likely the furthest from the truth. However fictional what you are about to read may be, you must also understand that every word is fact formed from authentic thought. I know it's confusing. Perhaps that is the point, to be confused.

To understand, I urge you to immerse yourself in the world of Eli Greene and imagine that you are them. It shouldn't be too hard to do so, mainly because Eli's life is so indistinguishable from your life or mine that you may question whether the book was actually written about you. I can assure you that it is. I can spoil it for you here and now: nothing extraordinary happens to Eli, just as nothing unusual happens to you or me. You will not learn some meaning to life within the margins of this book, but quite the opposite. It must be understood that no word in this book has meaning. That's the whole point, isn't it?

In contrast to any other existing document of human life, this book imitates what an actual existence looks and feels like. What is to be gained from this reading, however meaningless you may find it to be, is the mundanity of it all. I urge you to consider and reflect upon the sheer relative-ness you will feel while reading. And please, if you can prove me wrong by reflecting on yourself to Eli, well, what an extraordinary person you must be.

I.

BEFORE THE BEGINNING

CHAPTER ONE

The New Greene

My niece was born today. My sister relayed the message to me through my mother, who called me before class. They told me that she was beautiful. I wasn't able to make it to the birth or immediately following. She is 8 pounds 7 ounces, has beautiful blue eyes, and a full head of sandy blond hair. St. Mary's Hospital is six blocks from my school, so I will have to walk there. I shouldn't go during work hours, and the traffic on a day like today will be horrific, but I guess regardless, the experience will be an inconvenience in some way.

I had to cancel my last three classes, which I'm sure my undergraduate English students found incredibly taxing on their education. My Dean and colleague even reached out, seeming to be intensely frustrated with me, but there wasn't much I could do about it. I told him I would be back tomorrow, reassuring him. Frustration aside, he'll probably offer some form of a congratulation once he sees that I am celebrating this new birth. The thought of that conversation tomorrow aggravates me.

Lili is her name, my niece, and while I make my way out of the school, I try to picture her in my head. Blue eyes, sandy blond hair. I remember those summer days on the beach. I was watching the sand blow in waves over the water. Seated safely atop a new Toyota, I felt whole. What a fleeting and truthfully irrelevant feeling that was. It's a beautiful spring day today. The birds are chirping to each other throughout the scattered trees in the bustling city, and the sun beats down softly on their wings as they take flight. Spring offers birds a chance for rebirth, a new wind under their wings to guide them home or away from home.

I wish I could sit outside with a stack of papers and do my work instead of going to the hospital. I have essays to read and grade: blue eyes, sandy blond hair. I wonder if she will look anything like my sister or if she will look similar to every other baby to have ever been born. That's one thing about humanity: we like to think we are essential from the day we are born. Babies are always unique and beautiful in their own way to their parents, but everyone knows that a baby is just a baby.

I'm excited to see her. Or at least that is what I continue to tell myself as I saunter down the street. Being an uncle is a life achievement for a brother, so I have to be excited. It is a fulfillment of human existence to expand your family tree, let alone an expectation held by those around you.

I pass a large oak on the corner of 6th and Walnut. This tree has lived between buildings without proper sunlight for years, and yet it stands tall and proud, looming over me. As I stand waiting for the light to turn red, I observe a young couple in their early twenties sitting with their backs up against the old bark, holding hands and gently resting their heads together. Their eyes are closed, but I can see their mouths move softly, and I feel my blood begin to heat up in frustration. I want to know what they are discussing, but I am too far away to hear their voices. I imagine their conversation moving smoothly, along with vows of love and a long life together, and I giggle at the sentiment.

The crosswalk sign shifts from its usual red hand to the white walking pedestrian, and I take my first step onto the street. The cars yield to my crossing, and I wonder where all of their lives are leading them today and where their lives will lead them in the future. Of course, it isn't worth thinking or caring about because I will never see them again. I immediately excuse the thought and continue with my trek toward the hospital.

Two blocks from the hospital, my phone begins to buzz in my coat pocket. I removed the device gently, recognized immediately that it was my mother calling, and pressed the red button to end it. She is calling either to tell me something about Lili or to question why it is taking me so long to get there. She will speak with a tone of worry in her voice, expecting some disaster to have occurred that is to blame for my tardiness. I would have to answer her useless torrent of questioning with optimistic fervor and continue on my way. But I didn't want to do that, nor should I have had to. So, I continue to walk down the street, the blocks passing quickly by with my fast-walking pace.

"Isn't she gorgeous?" is the first thing my sister says when I walk through the hospital room doors. The process of finding the room was infuriating. I first had to find the birth ward; then, once I noticed I was lost, I had to backtrack to ask a nurse for directions. Twenty or so minutes later, I step into the room filled to capacity with my family. I gently push my way through to the center of the room where the bed is placed awkwardly, the head pushed up against the wall covered in wires and cords, all serving their own respective purpose.

My sister smiles, her blond hair pulled back in a messy bun, once she sees me. I notice the bags under her eyes and the strands of hair that fall from her face, and I wonder if she notices them. Her eyes are red from lack of sleep, but she glows with radiance.

"Eli," she says, and I reach for the child.

"Yes, she is gorgeous, Diana." She extends her arms out for me to grab Lili, and I wrap her in my arms—such a small body, just hours old and completely unaware of the corruption that accompanies life. I felt a sudden urge to protect and shelter this child from that corruption, but I quickly remembered that that was impossible. I steal a glance at my sister; in even a state like this- one in which a woman is known to be at her strongest- she looked weak. I almost wince at the thought of my sister's namesake, the Goddess of the Hunt. It is such a solid legacy to place on such a weak-willed woman. At least she was capable of this, I think to myself, qualifying the life in my hands as an excuse for my sister's fragility- perhaps even a hiccup in it.

Corruption and inevitable demise, whether through a loss of soul or body, are simply products of living. I silently scold my sister for her choice to bring this life into existence. I wish I could have children, but the thought of it offers too much of an ideal path, one that isn't actualized or proven through previous experience and observation. *When has the perfect path ever proven to work out perfectly for someone?* I think to myself, knowing the answer full well.

The light shines in from the window onto all of us, and I can't help but notice the particles of dust floating through the air. I move, in one swift motion, towards the chair in the corner of the room by the window. With Lili still in my arms, I carefully sit and nestle the bundle close to my chest. I look down at the child, sleeping silently against my heart, and I try to imagine the life my niece is going to live.

William, Diana's husband, appears next to me and rests his leg on the arm of the chair.

"Eli, thank you for coming," he says, gently brushing his daughter's hair from her face. I nod, a feeling of discomfort washing over me. I begin to wonder how else I am supposed to respond to that.

He continues to console his child while she is in my arms, and I can't help but want to return the child and take my place in the corner of the room. Oh, how I wish I could be reading *Grapes of Wrath* right now instead of this. Hell, I wish I could be reading anything instead of this. I take a deep breath in, and the hospital smell of cleaning chemicals burns my nose. Something about this- me holding a newborn baby, the fluorescent lights casting a yellowish hue on all of my family members, the misplaced smiles on everyone's faces- felt wrong. I can tell that my mother is observing me. I smile down at the little one in an attempt to please her. When I glance back up, she is nudging my father and whispering something in his ear. Now that the excitement of a new witness to birth had passed, everyone continued their side conversations while I sat, baby in my arms. Her eyes were already open, and she looked at me with an almost confused look on her face. She was wrapped tightly in a pink blanket, and a tacky bow brought by Diana was thoughtfully placed around her head, the bow, being different shades of pink, resting right above her right eye.

I tune out their conversation, and I begin to zone in on the beautiful face of the newborn. Once in her world, I feel innocent again. I feel what it means to be unaware of the corruption of life, of reality. Hours old, this child's life has already been planned out by her parents. Hours old, and I can see wrinkles already beginning to form on her forehead skin that should be new with plasticity. Even a child as young as she is no exception to life, no exception to the perversion that exists in this world, and I feel a tear begin to form in the corner of my eye. *What an odd feeling*, I think, *to cry over something that hasn't even happened.*

After that, everything seemed to go in a flash. Conversations continued, and people came and went. Aunt Susan and Uncle Benny planned a trip for their family, and they needed to get back home to pack for it. My mother, a short woman with fading brown hair that she replenishes with dye and dazzling green eyes that light up any room the minute she walks through the door frame, sits by my side for the remainder of the day. All I could think about was work and the catch-up that I would have to do with my students—that and, of course, those blue eyes and sandy blond hair.

CHAPTER TWO
Lili Is Her Name

Diana didn't want a girl. She didn't even like kids before meeting William. When imagining her life, Diana never expected that she would live her time existing on the dependence of others. Looking down at her belly after five months of pregnancy, she wondered if her life would ever be the same. She sat in her chair by the front window in the house she shared with William and pondered her future. The chair, now rickety from overuse, creaked underneath her. Diana rested her left arm on her belly as if it were a shelf, and she placed the other on her forehead. She wondered if, by some miracle, she could lose this thing growing inside her. The life that existed in her past would no longer be an option to live in her future because of this body existing within her very body, sucking out, day by day, another piece of her soul.

The future had seemed bright to Diana before pregnancy. Before William, even. But she knew that she needed to marry; it just suited her lifestyle. Marriage was the path for her; she knew it was. She began to think about Eli, who seemed, at least to her, to have the world figured out. Eli, the all-knowing. The sibling that Diana always felt compared to and yet never seemed to match. Existing in a world in which carelessness was the priority and where achievements were simply handed to people was the way in which her sibling seemed to live, and the mere thought brought goosebumps to Diana's body. She watched as her child pushed against the tight skin of her stomach, and she gently pushed back with her arm.

When Eli and she were children, they would play by the creek near their family home. The toads would croak from down below, the birds would chirp at the little ones from above, and life seemed so simple. Diana remembered Eli talking so calmly, with such confidence, about the life that they were going to live together. Eli was so confident in having children, a partner, and a career. Diana, on the other hand, was skeptical of her siblings' plans and began picturing a different life for herself, a life different from her siblings'.

Look at me now, she thought to herself, now rubbing her stomach with a gentle hand. The war between siblings had finally been won, but at what cost? Diana had a husband, a baby on the way and a career. She would- if she loved the child as much as her family tells her she would- quit her job and, in that way, lose the critical point to the triangle of life. Eli, on the other hand, had the career. Not the career that Diana wanted, either, so hadn't she some superiority?

The sun, now beginning to set, placed the light blue painted room ablaze with a fiery orange, and Diana knew that William would be home soon.

Maybe Diana began to think to herself; *maybe my life could go back to normal once this baby is born*, knowing full well that that concept was an impossibility for a woman like her. She had accepted her position, and so she shall be determined to live it out. Sure, she will go back to work if she so chooses, but life has been stripped from her in a way that can never be returned. Nine months of sitting in the rickety old chair by the window would lead anyone to inward insanity. Not only that, but Diana slowly felt her soul diminishing, her purpose becoming more and more invalid. *Or was it just transforming?* She would often think to herself in an attempt to remain optimistic. To stay in control of her life, her purpose had to change, hadn't it? Isn't that what everyone experiences throughout life? Nonetheless, her life was going to change, and she was not ready to deal with the consequences of her defaulted yet deliberate choice.

She rubbed her tummy softly, almost hoping that it would produce a genie to grant her three wishes, and she stood. Balancing herself with the help of the wall beside the chair, she moved slowly towards the stairs. Then, step by step, she made her way up into the nursery, and she began to cry.

She began to cry, not out of happiness or out of sadness, but for the reality in which she lived. She glanced at the wall across the room from her and, placed delicately above the crib, at her painting. A meadow of lilies, William's favorite flower, stood against the lush green grass and the earth. Lili, Diana decided in that very moment, would be the name of her child. She needed to exert her power in some way over this trauma so she would stand firm in thinking that this was the way to do it. The creek of her childhood, she remembered, had been lined on either side with various wildflowers. Daisies, Milkweed, and even Wild Rosemary and Sage would grow amongst the rocks and the trees. Diana would often beg Eli to lay with her in these flowers, just for a moment, to breathe in the beautiful scent and to feel safe and serene among them. Eli, intoxicated with a sense of superiority and dominance, would always immediately turn and walk towards the shallows where the toads would bathe in sunlight, yelling back to Diana that the flowers simply weren't worth their time or energy and that there were better things to do.

There's something almost metaphorical in that, she thought to herself, wiping the tears from her eyes. Something about that painting hanging above the crib, the name she had just chosen for her daughter, and the fond memories of her childhood turned her fear and sadness into something else. Had she finally found happiness? No, but what she had found was much more substantial.

She had found her power.

CHAPTER THREE

The Morning After

The morning after Lili's birth, life resumed as it always had before she was born. The alarm sounded at 5 am, and I knew I had thirty minutes to get ready. The routine, day by day, went as follows: alarm, coffee, shower, clothes, breakfast on the go. I enjoyed walking to work. I recognize this is a luxury that not many people have, especially those living in the city. I am one of the lucky ones, someone may say. My life has always been routine; it has always been planned, and the activities I partake in have always been fulfilled with their respective standard expectations. On occasion, I would change up my schedule and my routine, but it seems that nothing changes when spontaneity is incorporated. Of course, I shouldn't have expected much to begin with, and so I stopped having higher expectations long ago.

The alarm went off at 5 am, and I knew it was time to get up and have my coffee. The breeze from the open window above my desolate yet well-known queen-sized bed dissuades me from pulling the sheets from my body. I reach instinctively towards my bedside table, and I pull on the lamp's dangling thread to illuminate the room. In the drawer, I reach for my glasses and slide them on. The walls, a dark shade of blue, seem to close me in while also giving me all the space in the world. I make a mental note of these walls. I have seen the most intimate moments of my existence in the five years that I have shared with them, and yet they couldn't care one way or another about my feelings, my actions, or my aspirations. A man is like a wall but colder.

Finally, I find the strength to lift my legs out from underneath their cocoon of self-made warmth and I let them fall limply to the floor. Grounding them firmly against the hardwood floor, I stand and stretch. Suddenly, my phone begins to buzz from across the room. This seeming out of place and unusual, I make two quick strides to retrieve it and immediately recognize the caller as Diana.

"Eli," she breathes softly the moment I put the phone to my ear, "dinner tonight, my house? William is out on business, so it's just me and Lili."

I can hear the exhaustion in her voice. Trying to hide my annoyance, I force a smile.

"What time? I'm free after six," I respond with gritted teeth. My sister is calling me for company only when she needs me. If she hadn't had this baby, I think she probably would have gone a few more months before any contact.

"Six is perfect. I'll see you around then," she responds and promptly ends the call.

My brain begins to swirl with frustration and annoyance at this sudden invitation that I now have an obligation to accept. The invitation is fueled by desperation, exhaustion, and fear, not by genuine care for family love or sibling bonding. Instead, Diana needs constant recognition for her achievements, as we all do, and I, unfortunately, have fallen victim this time, ensnared in the crosshairs of her humanity. Blue eyes and sandy blond hair are what bring me back to a sense of reality, or perhaps it was the blue eyes and sandy blond hair that allowed me to escape to a sense of insanity, one that ignores the standard convention of realistic actions and emotions of the human species. It was these blue eyes and sandy blond hair that allowed me to continue on with my day, to put me back on track with my routine. Lili came to my mind after that phone call, and she remained in my mind until the moment I stepped up to the front door of my sister's house. It was at that point that I realized I had failed myself.

The day passed me in a blur, all of which contributed to the now failure that anything I accomplished would become of it. I only had two classes to teach, one of which I am piloting for the university. In between classes, I sat in for our Dean at meetings to discuss new aims for our zine and periodicals led by students as a representation of the work created by the school of English. The drama school was collaborating with us on this year's play, as well, which would be a reimagination of Hamlet- one of my favorites of Shakespeare's that I knew would not be given the justice it deserves in this new rendition. For this, however, was another meeting I had to sit in on in which discussions regarding the use of words were debated.

"Well, I just don't understand why we can't interpret them in our own way to make it more modern. Unfortunately, the reality is no one is going to come and watch if it's in the iambic pentameter. We have to make it engaging somehow" one of the students brought up. I sat quietly, Lili on my mind, with my eyes on the analog clock hanging above the closed wooden door of the conference room.

I allowed the reality to sink in that another human being had managed to become my motivation for the day, the blue eyes and the sandy blond hair. I had relied on a false power to get me through the day, and I felt defeated because of it.

I walk up to my sister's door and hesitate, with my hand wrapped around the freezing doorknob, as I begin to wonder if I should knock instead. I do, and almost immediately, Diana opens the door.

"Eli, I am so happy to see you. Can you hold Lili?" she says, urging me inside. Diana is empty-handed, but before I think to ask her where her daughter is, I glance into the living room on my left and see Lili lying on the floor, making little baby gurgle sounds.

"I'm not sure you should do that with her, Diana," I say, gently picking her up and cradling her against my chest. She nuzzles her way in between my breast and my armpit, and I can feel and hear her gentle coo. Diana is back in the kitchen preparing the meal for tonight, with no care for what I just told her or for the safety of her child. I move, with the child still in my arm, to the rickety rock chair in the corner, adorned with a stack of diapers. I quickly brush them to the floor and sit, feeling the wood strain against my weight. My eyes begin to wander anywhere but to the child in my arms. First, the portraits hanging on the walls create, and hopefully convince, any visitor of the actual comfort and security blossomed by the union of man and wife. The frames, a dark wood grain, no doubt from some expensive and obscure secondhand shop that tells a story beyond what any of us could imagine, all hang straight in lines across the wall, except one. When it catches my eye, it seems impossible to dismiss. And so, I linger here, on this tilted and imperfect frame housing a picture of Diana and William on one of their many Hawaiian vacations, the perfectly placed leis wrapped loosely around their necks. The ocean, a vibrant blue from the post-editing process, ripples gently in the background. And past that, the sun, just hinting of its existence on the skyline, washing the sky in shades of orange and red that contrast perfectly against the blues and purples of the ocean.

"One of your pictures is tilted," I blurt out regretfully. Fortunately, though, there is no response but a continued orchestra of pots and pans clanging uselessly around. It was the shock I needed to break the spell, and my eyes continued their journey. I took careful note of the fact that none of the frames on the walls held evidence of my relationship with my sister. In fact, none of my family lived within the frames among the walls of my sister's home. Slowly, my eyes fell on the books placed atop the coffee table in the center of the room. Around it was a set of leather furniture: a chaise lounge sectional, a loveseat, and a beautifully worn single chair with arms that puffed up all the way around it. I began to question why the books were placed there, in that specific spot on the coffee table. It is too far out of comfortable reach for leisure reading but too expensive not to have been read at least once. Or maybe it was not too expensive, as perhaps it was serving another purpose that I could not even fathom.

As this thought penetrated deep within me, my eyes again began to wander. I figured now would be a better time than any to relocate myself into the leather chair that seemed so welcoming. As I made this transition, and without wanting to, I stole a quick look at the child, and she held my gaze. Bright blue eyes, like the very tip of the ocean's surface, bore into me. I could feel her left hand reach for and grip the back of my arm while the other found its way into her mouth. In this, I got lost. *Is there any way to know what she is thinking?* I thought to myself. If my first degree taught me anything, it was that concrete information on childhood development was almost entirely nonexistent. But that was nearly fifteen years ago, so who knows what has changed. The room, still the dingy light blue color that it was when William and Diana had hastily purchased the house, seemed more comforting tonight than it ever had before. The soft sound of the child sucking on her hand; in the kitchen, I could hear Diana mumbling to herself.

"As I said before on the phone," she called from the kitchen, "William has just been so busy lately with work, and I figured it would be a perfect opportunity for us to get together." She paused. In an attempt to guide my attention to anything else, I put my forehead to Lili's and closed my eyes. I knew what Diana wanted to say next. *You know, William has just been doing so well at the firm. When I worked there, we were such a great team. We got virtually everything done in no time.* Diana- always bragging about the moments in life that should never really matter that much.

"You know, I was just visiting the firm a few weeks ago, Eli, and they practically begged to take me back. But you know how it is; I can't just go back. I need to grow and experience something better!" she exclaimed, and I could almost picture her throwing her arms up to the sky for dramatic effect. I began to lean into the leather chair in which I now sat, its burnt orange fabric gently pressing up against my bare arms. I could feel it beneath me settle against my weight as I myself settled into this comforting position of holding the child. Almost simultaneously, as comfort settled, I heard metal clang to the floor and Diana's screams, which forced my entire body to tense and break free from the safety of the leather.

CHAPTER FOUR

Dinner

"Everything is okay!" she screams from the kitchen.

Lili, now shaken by the loud noise, begins to crinkle her nose and squint her eyes. I know what is about to come, so I quickly start to rock her back and forth in my arms.

"It's okay sweetheart," I murmur, suddenly feeling a calming aura wash over me. The act of rocking a child back and forth comes naturally for me, knowing that it is in an attempt to let them know that everything is okay.

Before I think any more deeply about this thought, Diana appears in the doorway.

"The knife fell! I thought it was going to cut straight through my toe, but it just clattered to the floor. Silly me, I guess!" she says before noticing me and Lili. Almost immediately, she grabbed her from my hands and mimicked my behavior. *You can't fake love, Di',* I think to myself.

"It's okay, baby" she whispers, holding the baby awkwardly against her chest. She moves quickly back into the kitchen and I feel compelled to follow.

Diana's kitchen is filled with all the newest appliances. William bought her a completely new kitchen just a year ago in the hope that she would finally start cooking more for him. That's my guess, anyway. The marble countertops glisten as I walk in, and filling the main island is an array of food—mashed potatoes, chicken, biscuits, wings, gravy, the works. I make my way towards the food, pick up a plate, and begin delicately and strategically picking food from their respective custom-made hand-carved bowls and plopping it down onto my plate. While doing so, I start to doubt my perceptions of my sister. Maybe she really had done something good with her life. Learning to cook is good, right? I scold myself for the disrespectful thought.

"I figured KFC would be good, right?" she says, placing Lili in her cradle/baby carrier.

"Yeah, great!" I mumble, scooping a healthy portion of mashed potatoes onto my plate.

"Oh please, please sit," she says, scurrying over to the kitchen table and pulling out a chair for me.

Diana rarely has guests over, so I am not surprised that she doesn't know how to be a good hostess. She was never one for close friends, and so after college and marriage, she began to isolate herself as much as she could. I wonder if she's okay and if it'd be worth it even to ask her. *Probably not,* I decide, as I take my place at the seat she so graciously laid out for me. I always knew Diana to be over the top, but this situation is weird even for her. I began to speculate all of the reasons why she would have invited me over tonight, and now I am positive that my suspicion behind this dinner invitation was correct. I watch her as she places Lili in the booster seat beside the kitchen table, fumbling over the straps. I take a quick note of her hair, curled into perfectly brushed ringlets that fall just past her shoulders. She's wearing a diamond necklace, a gift from William, no doubt. Her dress, a beautiful deep burgundy, accents her figure nicely. *Why did she have to get the body,* I think to myself, jealous of her stunning figure.

She sits beside me at the table and crosses her legs quickly.

"Thank you for coming," she says. Her eyes remain on her plate, and I watch as she stabs at her chicken, tearing it to pieces with her fork. I can tell that she is nervous because her fork begins to fidget across the plate in a sporadic and irrelevant path, almost as though she has forgotten the primary function of the utensil.

"Eli, I have a favor to ask you" *here we go,* I think, "I want to… I need to go away for a little while. William will be back soon so he will take care of Lili, or I'll have mom look after her if William doesn't want to. But I need a break."

I want to laugh. To stand up and leave her house without saying a word. But that would be wrong. That would be fake, though it seems the most appropriate option in this circumstance. I wait for a response, deciding it's the best I can do.

Diana looks me up and down silently, pausing at my hands, both of which I have clenched at my sides, clinging to the edges of the chairs; I hadn't even realized I was so tense.

"You need to come with me," she finally says under her breath. I glance at Lili as she mushes mashed potatoes in between her fingers, and I envy her. In a moment of high tension and consequence, she remains innocent. She remains shielded from the annoyance of her mother--- for now. I wait before responding, hoping that the awkward moment will pass within seconds and we can continue eating. Diana's eyes fill gently with tears, and I know that she's playing with me. Her lips turn upward slightly into a forced smile, trying every trick she knows to get me to say yes.

Finally, I cave.

"I'll need to take work off. I don't know how they are going to find someone to take over my classes, but the administration and my Dean will give me an earful. What if I lose my job, Diana?"

Almost immediately, she counters with "Eli, you've been working there for over ten years, I am sure they can't do that much. You're a successful thirty-four-year-old, take a break with me."

I look up at the ceiling. She's right. Administration will deal with my absence, and my position will be waiting for me when I get back.

My students will love the chance to do nothing, but something felt off. What was I gaining by leaving my life behind? What life would I even be leaving behind?

Diana must see the gears working in my head, a skill she's mastered over the years growing up together, and I immediately mask the concern on my face.

"What did you have in mind?" I say, placing my hands on the table in preparation for deliberation.

I can't let an opportunity like this pass up. An opportunity to see my sister, to really get to know her and understand who she is; I can't let that go. So, I've decided that I have to put my life on hold, as I've done many times before, all in hope of adventure and of purpose in life.

CHAPTER FIVE

The Plan

Diana and I spent three weeks creating an itinerary for the trip. Three weeks were spent endlessly talking on the phone, through email, and over text. In other words, three weeks of Diana speaking over me, speaking for me, or just blatantly telling me what we were going to do. I had to tell the Dean of the College of Humanities that I was taking a month off, a sabbatical of sorts because that is how long we had decided to leave for. He was upset, but he understood for some reason, probably because he knew he didn't have any other choice.

When I first started working for Columbia almost eleven years ago, he advocated for me and helped me through the hiring process. He set up my meetings and my interviews and even mentored me through my first few years. Professor Greg Lillian, a phenomenal author and world-renowned professor, had decided to mentor me, a brand-new professor just out of graduate school. We spent a lot of time together for the first few years, long nights working on papers and editing for research. His office became my second home; without an office of my own at that point, I always loved taking my breaks between classes to read or write in his classroom. I respected him, and I put my trust in him—but that was an ignorant Eli.

His office, as I said, had become quite the sanctuary for me during those first few years at Columbia. Lined with books on either side, I always felt comforted by being surrounded by the authors I had been raised to love. The light from the far window would always shine through the curtains, which were always left slightly open, onto the dark oak desk in the middle of the room. Three chairs were placed awkwardly in a circle right by the door, all sitting atop a burgundy rug that I'm sure was purchased with a bright red color but had dulled over time from lack of care. The dust added to the comfort, somehow, and the smell of mildew and musty books always accompanied the piles of paperwork that we had to work through—late nights turned into early mornings, which turned into sleepovers. Oftentimes, I would find myself waking up ten minutes before a class I wasn't prepared for in one of those musty chairs. I'd have to sprint to class just to return back to that chair for another set of papers to grade. Then, wine and takeout were introduced into our routine; maybe that was our mistake.

We had been grading papers for an Oscar Wilde course I had introduced to the college and petitioned for. Dr. Lillian, having always advocated for me, pushed it through the board and allowed me to execute the curriculum with a class as a sort of practicum for me. I was about halfway through when he asked me to open the bottle for him.

"Let's take a break; we've been at it for hours, it seems," he'd said. I agreed, of course, because any distraction was a welcome one.

Three bottles later, he was on top of me. I don't remember the rest, but the rest doesn't really matter. After spring break, the welcome back wasn't so welcoming. I avoided his office, began walking home for breaks or after class, anything to avoid seeing him.

When it finally came time for me to confront him, it was clear he knew he had broken a rule within the university, a law within the state. I had the upper hand, and while I never intended to use it against him, no matter how much I wanted to, I knew that I could essentially continue living whatever life I wanted to live, and he would be forced to oblige. So, he accepted my request for an absence, and that was that.

Diana told William that I had planned a spontaneous trip for the both of us and had surprised her over dinner one night while he was away. His hatred for me seemed to grow ten-fold, surely not because I was taking his wife away from him but because it meant he would have to handle himself and the baby all alone.

The day came quickly, and Diana's excitement was overwhelming, so much so that it almost made me decide against the entire trip. We had agreed on a leisure drive up to our family cabin in the cape. From the city, we would rent a car and make our way up northeast towards the coast, stopping briefly along the way. It had been years since either of us, maybe even anyone in the family had taken the time to visit the cabin. I can't even picture some aspects of it anymore, and I find discomfort in thinking about its current state. Diana pulled up to my apartment building with the rental car, a 2015 black Ford Escape, and honked at me to come out. Luckily, I was already waiting for her at the front entrance because there was no way I would have heard her from the sixteenth floor, but how would she have known that, seeing as how she hadn't been to see my apartment since I moved in? I silently thank William for the car as I lug my suitcase down the main steps to the street.

"Are you ready?" Diana says, hanging her left arm out the driver's window. I nod my head as I open the back door, placing my suitcase hastily on the floor. The trunk is already packed with luggage, and I scoff at the thought of what could be inside.

Excitement surged through me, an unwelcome emotion, one that I have rarely felt since I was a teenager, and even then, I recognize now that during those times, I can't even validate that excitement as real. As I step into the passenger seat and get myself settled into my home for the next few weeks, Diana looks over at me.

"Let's go," I say shortly, slumping down against the leather seat. Diana hesitantly puts the car in drive, and it makes me wonder how long it's been since she has driven a car or had to drive for this long of a time. *Have I ever driven this far before?* The buildings of the city begin to pass faster and faster out of my peripheral view, and I start to block them out completely. *Maybe it will be good for me to get away,* I think, with the last shred of childhood ignorance that my mind possesses. The shred that, unfortunately, still longs to find a happiness that perhaps means something more significant than the person feeling it. The thought shakes free as Diana slams on the break. There, in front of us, stands a woman with a bouquet of flowers. She's screaming at us.

"What the hell is this?" Diana whispers under her breath before honking the horn.

I get out of the car and walk towards the woman. It seems as though the sounds around me cease to exist and all that comes into view is the woman and her flowers. She pushes them towards me, still speaking very loudly in a language I don't recognize.

"You are selling them?" I say, trying to speak over her. I hear a car honking somewhere behind me, but it's so muffled that I just find it annoying. In an attempt to end this encounter, I pull out my wallet and reach for a twenty. The exchange is seamless, and without another minute passing, I am back in the car with a bouquet of beautiful flowers: Carnations. They are nothing but sentimental, a simple promise I made to myself long ago and foolishly continue to follow. Diana begins to bicker with me, but before she can finish her sentence, I cut her off,

"Drive, Diana" I say, plucking one of the flowers from the bunch and putting it in the overhead visor. The rest I put gently on top of my suitcase in the backseat.

Suddenly quite tired, I close my eyes and after a while, I feel the car's tires hit the smooth asphalt below it and the road trip begins.

II.

THE BEGINNING

NOWHERE TO GO

CHAPTER ONE

Oscar

Oscar Wilde had a fascination with carnations: Green ones, to be specific. He often would wear them on his lapel in a silent representation of his sexuality. When I heard of this, I vowed to do the same. But of course, in today's society, what person puts a green carnation on the lapel of their blazer? Hell, who even wears a blazer?

Nonetheless, I took over his fascination and, for such, chose to always have green carnations in my office as well as in my apartment. It became a ritual for me, one that I shared infinitely for and by myself.

My mother came home one day, when I was about eleven years old, with three lilies—one for me, one for Diana, and one for my best friend Kell.

Kell had been my best friend since I was in preschool. She had, for some reason, always stuck by herself. We went to the park that day, just down the street from my house. At fourteen, she was already incredibly beautiful. On this day, she wore a blue and purple sundress, one that fit her body perfectly, unlike my own clothes, which would always fall from my limbs because my mom could never seem to find any that didn't look to be two sizes too big. Her brown hair, which had always been unkempt, was done up in a ponytail today. As we walked towards the park, our sanctuary away from home that offered a mystical load of opportunity, I glanced over at her glistening blueish-grey eyes. We shared the same eye color, though hers always shined brighter. She reminded me of the Goddess Athena, or perhaps it was Artemis, though, like both of them,

Kell always acted brave and with an aura of wisdom that was well beyond her years. I always admired this about her.

We arrived at the park, and almost immediately, she began to cry. She was holding the lily that my mother had bought for her, and for some reason, I wished I had brought mine. The flower, beautifully and blindingly white, looked wilted in her hand. I didn't know what to do. I should have done something. But, alas, we just sat there. I looked off at the trees swaying along the edge of the park while she cried silently beside me until, finally, she stopped.

"What is our life going to look like, Eli?" She asked me, and I smiled. Whenever we came to the park, our plan for the future was our favorite topic of conversation.

I picked a tall blade of grass and twisted it between my two fingers. "We're going to live in a huge house on top of the hill," I began as if this was a rehearsed script that we had practiced over and over again, "I'm going to be a writer! And you a... a doctor!" The excitement started to build in my chest, causing my throat to close up.

"And when are we going to get married, Eli," she said, and I froze. We had never talked about marriage before. She looked over at me and saw the skepticism on my face. The blade of grass between my fingers was essentially obliterated, turning my fingers a light green color from the chlorophyll. I picked up another blade and began twisting it once again.

"We can get married?" I asked finally, not fully understanding the severity of what she was saying.

"I'd like to." She said to me, but she looked away as if she were in the middle of two people, me on one side and someone else on the other. I dropped the blade of grass and reached for her hand.

What would they do in the movies?

She looked at me and smiled, the lily still in her hand. I knew, as well as I could have known at this point in my life, that I loved Kell. And maybe my life would have turned out differently if she hadn't left me. I leaned in, and I kissed her. It was an impulse decision, but my eleven-year-old brain had decided it was the most appropriate thing to do. She was surprised at first, I could tell, but I could feel her lips loosen and grow softer the longer they touched mine. When I pulled away, she was smiling an even bigger smile than before, and I smiled back. That was when I decided we were going to be married. We were going to live happily ever after, me and my first love. Perhaps not, though.

On our walk back, she told me about her father's return.

"My dad's back in town," she said, watching her feet as we walked. My gaze, one that had always remained on her face during our walks to and from the park, found it necessary to instead look at my toes, which came out from the flip flops I was wearing and clung to the outer edges; I was about to hit a growth spurt.

"My mom says that he's taking us west. I think that he is really going to; he bought the tickets and everything," she finally said after a few moments. We were almost home.

"You're leaving?" I said, feeling my cheeks heat up from sadness and anger.

"No. Well, yes. But not forever, Eli. I will come back after I turn eighteen, and maybe I'll go to college here!"

"What about our plans?" is all I could get out, feeling the water begin to well up in my eyes. I blink them away and feel my eyes begin to burn.

"They are still our plans! We aren't leaving until next year, but I wanted you to know." She said, and that was that. We both knew that there was nothing we could do about it, but even if we could do something about it, this was the chance that Kell had always been waiting for. She always talked about having her dad in her life, and I was excited that finally she was going to get it.

When we arrived back at my house, my mom was waiting for us. She looked concerned but didn't say anything, just welcomed us back home.

A knock on the door came soon after. It was Kell's father. Mr. Slanté was a big man, full on both arms with tattoos and endless muscles. He always interested me, even though I only met him twice in my life. His green eyes glared at us upon opening the door, and Kell froze. I could tell she was scared, but back then I had no clue why. She had just been so excited to see her father and spend time with him.

"We're leaving, Kallie. Let's go" he said, his voice hoarse. I had never heard anyone call Kell by her real name, but I guess her parents must have when she was at home. We had developed nicknames for each other almost immediately upon initiating our friendship because we both hated our given names. Kallie became Kell and I became Eli. My name stuck, for all of these years.

Without a word, she looped her fingers with mine and squeezed for a moment before letting go. It seemed as if I was watching a movie or as if my soul had left my body for a moment, and I no longer had any control over my actions. She released my hand, and it fell limp on my side. Her father reached for her and gently put his hand on her shoulder, urging her along. Once they were out the front door, my mom walked after them.

"Ronnie, is this really a good idea?" she questioned him, trailing closely behind my best friend and her father. I stood at the doorway, still feeling nonexistent; perhaps even numbness washed over my body. I couldn't explain it even today, but I don't like to think about it much. Mr. Slanté didn't return any response of expression to my mother, and he left her at the curb as he and Kell got in his car and sped off down the street.

This was the last time I saw my best friend, and I am not sure where she is or how she is doing. I reached out to her after high school, during the most challenging transition of my life, but I received no response. I wonder now if my experiences as a late teen would have reconciled themselves any other way had she been with me, but I feel content with how it all worked out. Wondering is just the mind's way of attempting to create a sense of purpose in the soul of humans; it's an imitation, a reflection, of what we perceive to be true. I've come to realize that wondering does no one any good, though I often question why I still do it.

I loved Kell, I honestly did, but my first heartbreak didn't come until much later. Had I known it was going to happen, I probably wouldn't have sulked for so long after Kell's disappearance. But again, that's what we do to cope after losing something or someone that, at the time, may seem gut-wrenching to us but is veiled under a harsh dose of reality; there is always something worse coming.

CHAPTER TWO

Twelve

While Diana drives through the outer rim of the city, a shooting pain runs through my left leg all the way up to the knee, and I wince. *The first time I understood that I wasn't invincible*, I thought, remembering the memory as I rubbed the pain away in the passenger seat of my sister's rented Escape. I knew that what I was feeling now was only phantom pain, a kind of pain that one feels when their subconscious reminds them of a physical pain, but not a pain from a physical event itself. It couldn't be a tangible pain because it happened years and years ago. Nonetheless, I feel it, and rubbing my leg only reminds me of the day I received the injury. My finger lightly traces the scar across the back of my leg all the way down to my Achilles tendon, almost completely faded from the years of care and covered by the forest of hair that has grown on my legs from lack of care.

It happened when I was twelve. Having still been showered in the fountain of youth and everything that comes along with it, I thought I was invincible. Diana was there, though I doubt she would remember the memory if I brought it back up. Or perhaps it was as traumatizing for her as it was for me, maybe for some other reason.

It was a cold and crisp winter morning; my family had decided to pack up and rent a cabin in the woods for Christmas. When I say family, I am talking about the entire Greene clan in one cabin. So, naturally, my sister and our cousins decided to explore the forest around the cabin. The forest during this season doesn't have much purpose because all of the trees are asleep, and the animals are asleep within them or underneath them.

This is the season that humans could probably find the most solace in; the quietness of the forest and its inhabitants seem to mimic the beat of a human heart. Steady, slow, and cold.

I chose to follow, trailing behind them, tormented with the thoughts inside my head rather than the bitter cold whistling above me. The trees offered a lot of shelter from the wind, but the air itself was thin and cold, as if we were inside of a vacuum that had been placed in the freezer.

Ronnie and Sam, my two older cousins, began to spout stories about witches and vampires who lived in the forest and loved to come out during the coldest days of the year. These stories interested me more than they scared me, but I feigned fear for their enjoyment and to ensure that they continued with their fables.

"My family has been coming here for years," Ronnie said, "so we know the way around." They were leading us to an abandoned shed on the lot of our cabin.

"One time, I heard a witch on the inside of the cabin," Sam said before pausing, clearly waiting for a reaction from me or Diana.

"And? What happened?" Diana said, her visible breath adding to the suspense of the moment.

"Well, I ran!" she replied exasperatedly, shrugging her shoulders, "I didn't want to get killed."

"There it is! Just up ahead there through that little clearing," Ronnie yelled at us while he bolted towards the shed, leaving us only one option— to follow him.

The shed shouldn't have even been given the name 'shed.' It was a small, decrepit little room with wooden walls, flooring, and a tiny little roof that offered no shelter from the weather outside. Snow had accumulated on the floorboards inside, and it was clear that years of weather had caused the decomposition and rot of the floor. We all peered inside. In the front of the 'shed' were two steps that creaked loudly as we all stepped up.

A tiny little standing area lay right before the door, and I noticed that, though the floorboards creaked here as well, they weren't half as bad as those inside the structure.

"You go first," I mumble to Ronnie, incredibly hypersensitive to the noises around us. The silence turns even the slightest noise into a deafening boom. Without thinking twice, Ronnie steps forward into the room while we wait outside. The door, hanging only on its bottom hinge, swings open quickly with a creak that resembles a deep roar.

"You gotta see this," Ronnie said, fear evident in his voice. I couldn't tell if he was faking it or not, and if I was being messed with, but I proceeded into the room without hesitation. Something came over me, and for some reason I suddenly wanted to be in the room, I needed to see what it was Ronnie wanted me to see. I push past my sister and my other cousin and, once in the room, I see it.

In the corner to the left of the door is a small mattress, made out of I-don't-know-what, with a small square pillow that at one point was white but had been stained with spots of yellow and brown. Pushed up against the wall was a small blue blanket, hand-knitted, with strings of yarn coming out of the original stitching.

"Look at this," Ronnie said, walking over to the mattress and picking up the small blanket with two fingers. I hadn't noticed Diana and Sam come in, though I knew that they were right behind me.

From under the blanket, he pulled out a bottle of liquor. With a massive smile on his face, he lifts it up for all of us to see.

"Let's just go back to the cabin," Sam whispers to my sister behind me, and I'm about to turn around when Ronnie twists the cap off of the bottle and tosses it to the ground.

"Not before we try some of this," he responded, knowing full well that his sister wasn't talking to him. I took a step forward, and the two behind me stayed in their place, frozen in time.

Kids will do stupid things all the time; it is a part of life, and learning how to live it. And, of course, kids will have regrets when they become adults for the stupid things that they did when they were kids. But, and I hope this is true, it is rare for a kid to live with a constant reminder of their stupid acts. That day, while standing in that small room that we called a 'shed,' was a day that I can never forget. It was all due to the crow; that's who I should be mad with. The crow that tore my leg apart somehow ripped shreds of skin away from muscle and muscle from bone. A crow that, even today, left me numb in part of my leg from tendons and nerves that the doctors somehow couldn't or didn't know how to stitch up and replace.

My sister and Sam ran first, and then Ronnie. But I wasn't scared, not yet, anyway. No, I was watching the wood fall around me. I don't know what came over me that resulted in spooking me or what it was that even spooked them, but when the crow landed on the roof of the shed, its slight touch drove a wooden plank to fall to the ground near the mattress; they bolted. And I came soon after.

"Let's go!" Diana screamed, running out the front door and jumping off the front standing area, skipping the steps that we had used so tentatively as we made our entrance.

I was the last one out, so I guess that was my mistake, not to have known that the pressure of their weight on the wood would loosen some nails or crack some of the fractals within the wood, ripping apart the fibers that hold it together, much like my leg. Finally, when I did reach the steps, the sky seemed to erupt into a red, the color of a dark cherry being burst with the hard clench of teeth. Suddenly, it seemed, I was two feet shorter, and I was incapable of escaping the mattress, the falling wood, and the crow; that crow that most likely watched with a smirk on its beak, knowing that it had caused so much destruction.

What were my options? To scream for help? To sit and wait until they noticed I was hundreds of feet behind them with my leg caught in a wood trap?

I chose the latter. My voice was stripped away from me anyway, most likely from shock. So, I waited there, with my leg filling the enclosed area below with a pool of red liquid, as I watched the sky shift from the darkest cherry to the lightest and most beautiful color of pink cotton candy. I stayed awake; it's not like I fell unconscious or some bullshit that we always read happens in movies or books. My mind didn't shut down, and my eyes didn't feel heavy. But I don't remember what happened after that because I willingly chose not to.

The only thing that matters, now, is that I am sitting in a car, a good twenty-odd years later, still rubbing away the crow's insignificant act that changed my life forever. Never was it I who changed my life, but always life that changed itself for me. A person, a place, or a crow.

But, never me. And some people may realize that and find that it causes them anxiety or fear that life has taken control over them rather than the other way around, but not me. I welcome life's changes, and I don't care that I have made no conscious decisions that led to changes in my own life.

CHAPTER THREE
Roadside Assistance

Diana and I have been on the road for over two hours now, though it seems we haven't made any progress. Sure, we're almost out of New York, but our travels have existed in a particular silence that is almost excruciatingly frustrating—two hours in a car with your sister, making small talk. Probably not the way most siblings would spend a road trip together, but here we are, breaking stereotypes.

"How many more hours until our first stop?" she says, motioning with her right hand to the GPS she's positioned on the dashboard. We had planned to stop at a small motel before nightfall so that we didn't have to drive in the dark. I reach for the small machine.

"forty-five more minutes," I say. She looks over at the GPS in my hand, and I feel my frustration begin to rise. *Why would you ask me to look at the time if you were just going to check it anyway?* I think to myself.

She grabs the GPS out of my hand, which sets a whole series of events into motion. I wasn't expecting it, though; who would expect a dog to bolt out onto the freeway? I don't even have the chance to warn her before I hear the most guttural screech erupt from the brakes on the car in front of us. Diana whips her head back towards the road, dropping the GPS down in the center console.

"In 40 miles, take Exit 127," the robotic voice says, muffled by the crack that it fell into. The dog, lying idle on the lane markings between the far left and the middle lane, looks oblivious to the chaos it's causing. Diana, in an attempt now to avoid the car in front of us, swerves hard to the right, sending me flying towards her side of the vehicle. She levels us out on the shoulder before slamming her foot down on the brakes. The carnation I placed overhead ejects itself from the visor, and it flies through the air, landing somewhere far back.

"Stop the car!" I say in a firm voice, bracing myself for the median we are about to hit on my side of the car. Before we hit, though, we heard a considerable POP, and the vehicle shifted its weight so much that Diana was now sitting inches below me.

A flat tire.

We finish rolling to a stop and I immediately press the button on the dash for our hazards. I can tell Diana is too embarrassed to look at me, so I reach out for her hand.

"It's okay. We are okay," I say, squeezing her hand. There are times when we have to be strong for each other, and this has to be one of those times. I feel her hand shaking in mine, and I squeeze tighter to calm her nerves.

After a few minutes, she looks up at me. The only sound in the car comes from our blinking hazards. Her eyes are bloodshot, but I see no tears coming down her face.

"Let's switch seats, okay? We have a flat tire, so we'll need to take the next exit and we can figure it out from there."

Without another word, she pulls the handle on her door and takes a step out of the car. I can tell she is still shaky, but I know that it's just adrenaline and the aftershock.

I make my way to the driver's seat and wait for her to buckle into the passenger before I start the car up again. With the hazards still on, I slowly re-enter onto the freeway, and I drive with my hands firmly placed on the steering wheel. The drive between the accident and our next exit felt excruciatingly long. With a flat tire, I was forced to reduce the car's speed to 40 m.p.h. Diana, sitting in a fetal position beside me, gently whimpers and shakes. I don't know how to comfort her, and it makes me annoyed. I wish she would just stop crying and deal with the situation, but I guess she just isn't like that. My frustration builds the longer we stay on the freeway, letting my thoughts run rampant of all the times I've had to be the protector of my sister and how I've never felt the favor returned to me.

"Thank you" she mumbles, but I ignore her. I take the exit, after what feels like hours but was most likely less than three minutes, and the search for a gas station begins. Thankfully, after only a few turns, I turn the car into a run-down, seemingly in the middle-of-nowhere, altogether gross gas station, and I turn the car off in the middle of the lot.

"You'll have to call the rental place," I say, "can you go do that?"

She nods and opens her door, stepping out slowly and stretching her arms. I open my door as well, but only for fresh air. I turn my back to Diana while she goes into the convenience store, and I notice, with my legs dangling on the outside of the driver's seat door now, that there is a group of guys huddled around something on the other side of the street. *I didn't notice them there when I first pulled in*, I think.

I want to call out to them and ask what they're doing or looking at, but I decide against it. It doesn't really matter; their business is not my business. I notice one of them glance my way, and I choose to glare back. He kept eye contact with me, and I suddenly realized we had entered into a battle, a childish staring contest. I decide, then, that I will not give in to such childish games, so I stand and stretch my legs, ignoring his burning eyes.

Out of my peripheral, I see him attempt to cross the street. After a few trucks pass by, he trots across in the awkward walk-run that people often do in order to get from one side of the street to the other, and he stops just feet from me.

"Hey, you got a flat tire?" he says, still looking at me. I can tell he is observing me, trying to decide whether or not I'm human, trying to gauge my reaction.

"Yeah, we just got in an accident a mile or so back," I say clearly, still stretching. He eyes me up and down, and I choose to do the same. His eyes, a striking blue, stand out above everything else. They look all too familiar. I begin to wonder if he got that from his mother or his father. He is wearing a white t-shirt wrapped loosely around his frame, which I can only suspect is slightly toned. His dark brown hair, styled quite well, shines in the sun and blows gently in the wind.

He can tell I'm observing him just as I can tell he's observing me.

"Do you need any help?" he offers, taking a step closer. Before I can respond, I hear Diana exiting the convenience store, the door sounding with its cliché bell ding.

"The rental company says they can't do anything except send a tow, and that'll set us back at least a day from our plans," she says, walking back to the car, "so what should we do?"

"Where are you headed, if you don't mind me asking?" the man blurts out almost immediately. My mind flashes red, and my irritation rises.

"We have a family cabin out on Cape Cod, just speaking a few weeks out there," I replied plainly.

"Well, we're just outside of Dartmouth, so you're only a few hours' drive from the cape. Do you need a ride? It doesn't take me much farther out of my path, and I have no problem doing it."

I want to say: *We don't need a stranger offering up their car to us, thank you. We're adults; we can figure it out.*

I settle on: "No, that's alright. We will figure something out. Thank you though" completely neglecting to answer or even acknowledge his question.

"Truly, I don't mind!" he says, now holding his keys out to us.

"Well, that is kind of you! We are actually trying to make a whole trip out of it so we were hoping tonight to stop in Fairhaven before picking back up tomorrow and heading over. You sure you'd want two strangers to join you in your car?" Diana says. Her ignorance astounds me.

With a smile, he takes a few more steps towards us. We're now sitting in a little triangle, like school kids waiting for their bus.

"You seem like a pretty trustworthy couple. At least let me help you get to where you're going in Fairhaven, then hopefully someone there can help you get a new car, or the tow company can get you back on track," he asks again, "As I said, I don't really have any burning demands at the moment, so I'm yours to use at your disposal."

"Well, I suppose we would love the company, wouldn't we Eli? My name is Diana, nice to meet you" She extends her hand to our new friend, the stranger.

"Nice to meet you, Diana," he says, taking her hand, "I'm Hudson... Hudson Carver. A spontaneous trip sounds like exactly what I need right now. I provide the car; you provide the company. That alright with you?" he looks over at me now, his hand still extended. He expects me to just take his hand in mine and move on like this is all so normal and appropriate. My anger rises. I turn and reach back in the car, pulling out one of my bags.

Turning back around to face him, I say, "Where's your car?" and he smiles.

CHAPTER FOUR

Thirteen

I was thirteen the first time I trusted a man who didn't share the same blood as me. This isn't to say that I should, or do, trust any men who do, in fact, share my blood, but I did at the time. The summer had just started, and so had my transition into adulthood. I was told that I was a late bloomer, that it ran in the family, but I didn't really care about it either way—that type of stuff didn't interest me until years later. As for the heartache from Kell's disappearance, it finally subsided, leaving behind a small space within my mind that pulsed with the nostalgia of the memories we shared. But that was it. That was all I had left of her, anyway, so it did not take much work for my young mind to compartmentalize, albeit unknowingly, what I had once felt was such an impactful relationship.

I was sitting on the grass watching my neighbors, a group of boys around my age, play a pick-up soccer game on the field. I watched them, and I pretended not to care when they glanced my way. Some of them chose to take their shirts off, and I wish I had that luxury. I was a chubby kid, a bit overweight, so the thought of summer clothes never appealed to me. I fingered at the green blades beneath my feet and silently reveled in being close to the earth. Our local park, about a ten-minute walk from home, was a popular spot for most kids in the neighborhood for many reasons. It was outlined by tall fir trees that were not only perfect for climbing but also gave refuge to the beautifully grassy soccer field, sandy baseball pit, and kid's play center. The swings, two of them, swayed gently in that wind, their rusted metal handles twisting up gently and untwisting in a playful opera of sounds that brought both nostalgia and a tinge of annoyance to my ears. It was almost as if the creaks were calling me to them, to stand up off the grassy earth and sit again against the plastic-coated metal seat.

Instead, I watched for hours that day as the neighbor boys played game after game of ball. As a disguise, I would raise my summer reading up to my face and peer over it like a spy in a cliché undercover mission movie. When the sun fell, and the park lights flickered on, everyone knew it was time to go. I would usually leave before then, but this summer was different, and I had no friends with whom to spend my days. So, I figured I would stay—spend a little bit longer on the grass. And, as the sun fell and the moon rose, I started to find comfort in the darkness, comfort in the stars and the little light that they provided.

Weeks passed, and the routine remained the same; I would go to the park and watch the boys play their games, and once the sun fell and everyone at the park made their way home, I would stay. Invisible, I always felt, during this summer. I liked it that way because it gave me more time to think, more time to observe, and more time to learn. These were things that kids my age never liked to do. But one night, I watched as the boys all said their goodbyes to each other and rode off on their bikes or walked home; one of them stayed behind. Laying with my back on the quilted blanket I had started to bring to watch the stars, I flipped around to lay on my stomach so that I could watch him. He stood for a few moments and then began walking back towards the field, juggling his ball back and forth between feet. He had skill, I could tell, but in the darkness, I couldn't quite make out his face.

I flipped back over on my back to resume my stargazing. The beautiful thing about the stars, I came to realize, is that they are always there. Of course, they shift and become brighter on some days and dimmer on others, but every night, the North Star remains in its place, and from it, I can connect the dots of the Big Dipper. I remember wishing, at that age, and vowing to myself that one day I would see all of the star's constellations one day. I still love the stars and the darkness that surrounds them but for a different reason.

So, getting lost in the stars again, I felt myself begin to doze off. This was always my signal to go home when I started to feel the night taking over my body and putting weight on my eyelids. So, I begin to stand up, when I hear footsteps behind me.

"Oh, are you leaving?" a boy's voice says.

I whip my head around quickly and notice immediately that it's the boy who stayed behind, with his soccer ball nestled in the nook that his body naturally makes between his ribs and his hip bone. He holds it in place casually with his left arm, and I can see now up close that the hair on his arms is standing on end, producing small little bumps across his skin.

"Yeah, I should probably be getting home," I say, finally.

"Hey, aren't you, Eli? You come here pretty often, huh?"

"It's a nice place to read. What's your name?" I respond, feeling a little surge of confidence.

"I'm Abraham, but my friends call me Abe. Nice to meet you. Mind if I sit?" he says, putting his ball down.

I scoot over a bit so he can have some of the blanket, and I pick up my sweater and pull it over my head quickly.

"How come you haven't gone home yet?" I speak

"Well, my dad never really gave me a curfew, so I like to avoid home as much as possible. And I saw that you've been staying after everyone left, so I figured I'd introduce myself. That cool?"

"That's cool," I say, and in an attempt to seem uninterested, I lay back down and look at the stars. He lays down, too. We sit there in silence for a bit, and I almost enjoy the company. It's nice to have someone there with me during a summer that I felt alone during the majority of.

"We should hang out" he finally says, and it catches me off guard. I can tell he's nervous, because I look over at him and he won't make eye contact with me, he keeps his gaze fixated on the stars. *I wonder which star he's looking at?*

"We're hanging out now, aren't we?" I say, my cheeks turning red. Thank goodness it's dark out, or else he would know that I am blushing.

"Well, yeah, I guess you're right. But I meant during the day," he says, trailing off. "Would you want to?"

I notice that the North Star shines a little brighter tonight.

"Sure, we can do that."

CHAPTER FIVE

Carver

*H*udson was an easy man to read. They all were, now that I know what to look for. Once we hit the road again, cruising at the exact speed that the limit of the law asked for, we were able to put the gas station behind us. We transferred our belongings fairly seamlessly, with the help of Hudson Carver, and now sat in his truck; Diana was in the back seat, and I, of course, was sitting next to our savior. We spent about a half hour in silence until finally, I saw him look intently around the car- searching for something to spark a conversation.

"What's with the carnations?" he said, looking at the bouquet that I had moved and tucked gently in the bag at my feet. I felt a sudden urge, as I often do when someone chooses to ask me a question that refuses to involve them, to snap back at him. Instead, I feigned an interest in the weak attempt at conversation.

"They're just beautiful flowers. We bought them from someone off the street back in New York." I said, pushing them closer to my seat with my left foot.

He looked over at me, one hand so carelessly on the steering wheel and the other on his emergency break- like he was going to use it to change gears in his car with automatic transmission. I wondered if this was a habit of his, putting his hand where a stick shift would be, and continued to think about whether he has ever driven a manual car. *Why does it matter?* I push the thought aside.

I can tell he knows my response is entirely sub-par, even for me, but I hope he doesn't push it any further. Instead, he just looks back to the road and speaks indirectly to Diana.

"You ever heard of Oscar Wilde?" he says, not moving his eyes from the road.

"Yes, I have! He was a writer, right Eli?" Diana says from the backseat, shuffling almost uncomfortably because I know this is not her area of expertise but she will do anything to keep a conversation with Hudson going. I nodded my head, "that's right, he was." I mumbled, still practicing disinterest in the conversation, and now a bit of ignorance to the topic of the conversation. *Where is he going with this?*

"It's kind of funny" he began, "those flowers remind me of something Oscar Wilde used to do. Eli, I'm surprised you don't already know this" his lips curled into a small smirk. He was catching me in a trap I clearly had no clue I was falling into, like some sort of game of cat and mouse. I always thought the mouse was more intelligent than the cat.

"He would use green carnations as a symbol for homosexuality- like some sort of code," he continued, "and if I'm going to be honest with you, I thought it was a bit too cliché, almost too symbolic. Why a carnation? It seemed like there could have been something more concrete and simpler."

"Why would you say that? There's a reason for its complexity. If it weren't complex, there would be no purpose for it. We wouldn't be, at this moment, talking about it if it were just simple and concrete." I had fallen into the trap. There was no way to escape now; I had to commit.

He didn't skip a beat before saying, "Well, in its simplicity, don't you think it could hold more purpose? But I do believe you're right about one thing. In simplicity, there's no grey area. It's just black and white, so we wouldn't be here arguing. Right?"

This is clearly what he wanted. Who the hell was this guy? Who just meticulously starts a conversation about the complexity of simplicity while knowing I'll take the bait? I couldn't respond to him because responding would give him exactly what he wants but I also can't not respond because he needs to know the truth; my truth, but the truth nonetheless.

"You seem to have truly thought this out," I respond, content with my final contribution to the conversation.

"I do tend to think a lot when I drive, and I drive a lot. So, yeah, I have thought this out," he says plainly, gripping the wheel now with both hands. The road ahead of us is bare beside us, and the few trucks that we quickly pass by. On either side of us, we pass houses, cities, and fields, and it quickly becomes monotonous. I begin thinking about Connecticut and how, even though I've never been before, it looks so similar to all the other places I've visited or lived. There's no real difference between the places, the people, and the experiences. It's all very similar- intoxicatingly so. I know Diana, slightly slumped onto her seat belt sleeping away, would disagree with me, but I can't help but wonder if Hudson is feeling the same way. He seems to have at least an ounce of intelligence in him, though no sane person would willingly offer up their car, and more valuable to people- their time- for anyone, much less two complete strangers. I should have questioned these motives earlier, and I reprimand myself for not doing so, but I know we are way too far deep to turn back. Whether we want to be or not, this adventure includes Hudson Carver. This journey, however relatively basic it will turn out to be, will have his name and face etched into it. My mind quickly jumps to a single thought: was he meant to come into our lives? And I almost laugh from even entertaining the idea. The answer to that? Of course not. It just happened. I hope he knows that.

CHAPTER SIX

Fourteen

Abe and I grew really close after that night at the park. We stopped going to the park and instead found our own spot to watch the stars at night. When we found out how close we lived to each other, we basically became inseparable. He became my best friend; I trusted him, and he trusted me.

It was a random day when he called; school was out and I knew I had nothing to do, but looking back on it always leaves me with a sense of urgency I can't quite place. Almost as if then I was ignorant of something I know now I needed to do that day, but clearly even I now couldn't put my finger on it.

"Hi, Mrs. Greene, may I speak to Eli?" and my mom picked up.

"Sure, Abraham, one moment." My mom always called my friends by their full names after Kell left. "Eli! Abraham is on the phone for you."

Sitting on my bed, reading, I carefully put my bookmark in its place and set my book down on my bedside table. I walked out into the hallway where we always kept our upstairs home phone, and I picked it up.

"Hi, Abe, what's up? I say

"We're going to the mall in fifteen minutes; my older sister already agreed to drive us. Be ready!" he said

"Okay, but…" the line cut out, and he hung up on me. Abe always liked to keep things spontaneous, but never this spontaneous. It intrigued me at this age.

Quickly, I start my scavenger hunt, running around the house in search of my shoes and a new shirt. It didn't hit me until after I'd gotten into the car that I accidentally forgot to ask my mom if it'd be alright for me to go.

It took about three minutes from the time I left my house for them to arrive. I heard them before I saw them, their car screeching against the paved road. When they pulled up, Abe jumped into the back seat and opened the door for me.

The car, a beat-up Ford Taurus that was most likely passed down through their family, was littered with fast food wrappers and plastic water bottles. I had to wade through the garbage and push what I could to the floor before getting comfortable in my seat.

"Why are we going to the mall?" I whispered, after a few minutes listening intently to Abe and his sister go off about the smallest little thing.

"Just to hang out; I wanted to go to that new coffee shop that just opened," he replied.

That had become our thing: coffee shops. This isn't to say that coffee shops were exclusively "our" thing, but we made it mean something to us. Every new coffee shop that we could get to, whether by bike or by ride, would be rated by us on our list of favorites. We'd frequent our top three and go back to visit the others every once in a while to see if it has gotten any better.

"The new one?" I asked, confused.

"Yeah, it just opened in the mall, right next to the frozen yogurt place."

"Which one?" I giggled.

I would have done anything back then to get even the slightest smile from Abe. He smiled, but it was a traditional Abe smile; the kind that gently is lifted on the left side while the right kind of hangs in place. His dimples show, but it's as if it takes the least amount of effort for him to present something so beautiful.

His eyes, green and glistening in the midday sunlight, radiated through me.

"We're here. You sure you don't want me to tell mom to pick you up?" Abe's sister calls out, seemingly from a far distance. I snap myself out of the haze.

"No, we'll be okay," he replies, already hopping out of the car. I follow diligently.

We had to weave our way through the crowds of people, so we made our way slowly towards the location. Mindless walking led my mind to think about how grateful I felt to have a friend like him. Nothing in our lives, at this point, mattered except for our silly coffee shop ratings, and it was pure bliss. We didn't need to attach feelings or labels to each other; Eli was Eli, Abe was Abe, and Eli and Abe were Eli and Abe; nothing more needed to be said.

"Definitely my favorite so far," Abe said, tipping his coffee cup towards the sky, devouring every last sip.

I nodded my head, sitting back in one of the leather lounging chairs and grabbing my belly.

"Agreed. How'd you find this place?"

The shop had vintage hanging light bulbs strewn all across the ceiling, beautiful dark oak furniture and bar seating. The walls were wooden slabs with holes cut out for hanging wall plants, which seemed as if they had lived for years already in this same spot. We sat in the corner, both in a comfy leather chair. Abe rested his feet up on the round coffee table while I continued to sink further into my seat, feeling fully content with my coffee *and* my company.

"Well," he replied, "I heard about it around town being opened up in the mall sometime during the spring, so I did some research. I found out that they have a ton of them all over the state, but this was their grand opening here, in our town. So, with my master detective skills," he smiles and pauses, as if for dramatic effect, "I looked at our ratings for all of our other top favorite shops, and it seemed to be that this would be one of your favorites. I'm pretty glad it just so happened also to be mine."

Did I love him? I thought just then. Could it be possible for me to love like this?

I watched him settle deeper into his chair and I wished that I could sit with him, feel his skin against my own with the leather between us. He moved the hair out of his face and looked at me.

"So, how are we feeling about our rating? You know the drill: atmosphere, people, coffee, and conversation. Go," he said, a smile beginning to peek through the corner of his lips.

"How can I rate conversation when we haven't even started talking!" I said in a tone that made it clear I wasn't looking for a real answer.

Most tables were full, and I took a moment to observe the people sitting around me. A man and woman sat with their laptops open to my right, and a group of teenagers sat around a small circular table to my left. In front of me, what looked to be a couple sat in deep and quiet conversation, looking profoundly and almost longingly into each other's eyes. The shop was by no means overwhelming with noise; however, it was clear that this was a gathering place for all types of people: intellectuals, business people, a fun teen hang out, and me and Abe. We don't fit into a type; at least, we didn't then.

I can tell he is eyeing me quizzically, trying to read my mind through the glances around the room I am making. I look at the hanging vintage lamps again and notice the dust already beginning to settle on them. *Only a few weeks*, I think to myself, *and the furniture is already collecting dust.* I know it didn't mean anything, but it still succeeded in putting an unfortunate pout on my face.

"What is it?" Abe reacts almost immediately, "Too much greatness for one brain to handle?"

I laughed and took a sip from my coffee.

"You're right, you got me. I'm giving it 10s across the board. Even so, the people seem boring, the coffee is already getting cold, and there is dust piling on the lamps above us- I'm basically dying over here from hay fever!" I joke, knowing it will light a fire inside him.

"And again, no conversation as of yet between the two of us has sparked my interest." I raise an eyebrow curiously, waiting for his remark.

This is how a typical weekend looked for a while: Abe and I joking around at coffee shops and discussing the hard truths of the world. That day, we delved into more conversation than I've had combined with anyone in my adult life and a grasp on life that was so full and, selfishly, ours. I can still taste that life. Every time I lick my lips, the taste of sweet sugar cookies brings me back to those coffee shop days. It is an odd comparison, I'm aware, but the nostalgia is what I am aiming to get at: the artificial taste of something good but not that great.

CHAPTER SEVEN

The Holy Trinity

I pretended to sleep, closing my eyes and letting the gentle rolls of the tires against the asphalt lull me into a pseudo-relaxed state. As it always does, my mind drifted to places beyond my seat. The thoughts I had seemed to float from my seat to the car, to the road and city we were driving through, all the way until they reached the entirety of the universe. And in that thought, I stayed. I stayed thinking about the universe and its creation and how, for me, our creation had always been seemingly irrelevant.

The dilemma of God was born in me during my later teenage years. Before then, I was awash in the typical propaganda that was unequivocally accelerated by the musings of family members.

On the Tuesday of my first communion, I sat in the church pews awaiting my name and the group of twenty or so other kids my age to be called up to the altar. The altar, which I later learned supposedly held the left ear of its patron saint, sat in the front center of a two-leveled platform in which about thirty people could stand. The platform, a dull green carpet, covered both the steps and the entirety of the floor. On each corner of the hexagonal floor, a candle stand stood erected about six feet, and the altar boys were making their beeline directly to them. I knew my cue. After the altar boys lit their candles, the choir sang, and our father asked us to join us at the altar. I could never, even to this day, get over the feeling one got while sitting in those wooden pews and looking directly up at our high ceilings that bathed the walls of the church in natural light from the sun above, shades of all different colors from the stained glass casting beautiful images across the faces of Jesus and Mother Mary.

As we were called to pray, I was motioned to exit the pew and join my classmates near the altar. I was placed beside the father, who grabbed my small hand in his own and began the prayer for everyone in the congregation. It was a short while, or so it seemed, and even though I couldn't have been any older than five or six, I knew not to squeeze too hard against the father's hands, veiny and wrinkled as they were. The rest of the day went in a blur. I was given gifts, food, and praise by family and friends of the family, and I remember it fondly.

Flash forward about ten years. God had all but abandoned me, it had seemed, and after the death of my grandfather, I felt even more alone. Once the one who held our family together, my grandfather was my God until, of course, he wasn't. He was always one thing: strong. Having been a war veteran, as well as a man who had overcome such hardship in his childhood and early life as a married man with multiple children, he always seemed to me something otherworldly. Then, he got cancer. It was probably the most human thing he could have done in my eyes as a fourteen-year-old. Even then, however, his presence in my life remained and shook me with its ethereal sense. I felt I had a duty to him to not only be a grandson worthy of his attention but to be a man worthy of carrying his name.

And so, after his death, after he died and God died with him, I figured it was the only thing I could do to honor him and prove my worth to him, wherever he may be, to get confirmed into the Catholic church. Did I believe in God suddenly again? No. But, I had convinced myself he wanted it, and so it had to be done.

The confirmation was not as memorable as the communion, maybe because my innocence was just about lost to me at that point, and yet I pushed through. I ran through the motions I was expected to run through, and I was anointed as a confirmed member of the Catholic church. It was one day, years after Grandpa had died, and I was sitting on the back porch with my dad when he looked at me and said,

"Why did you choose to be confirmed? You know your mother, and I wouldn't have minded either way."

I looked up at the sky, darkened by the change of the suns position around the earth and yet still somewhat unpolluted by the bustling city just twenty minutes away. The stars, begin to shine more and more clearly by the minute, illuminate my pocket of vision. I picked one and tracked it, refusing to lose sight of it.

"It was for me. And for Grampy," I said, slowly, "I guess I wished that maybe being confirmed might then mean that the truth of religion would be confirmed for me. If that makes sense."

"It doesn't," he said and returned back to his beer. My eyes stayed fixed on the star, my one star that stood out among the others. I swear if I stared long enough at it, all the others disappeared from view. And yet, as I unfocused my eyes, there they all were again. And I was back, unsure of anything.

It was this unfortunate thought that brought me back to the car. Back like a whistling wind that has traveled the ends of the earth, the ends of the universe more likely, and hesitantly or begrudgingly returned into my mind. It had explored, but it had returned empty-handed. I knew we would be there reasonably soon; it couldn't be more than a few hours now. I look over at Hudson, who has his right hand on the steering wheel and his other resting against the window. His hand sits nestled within his hair, and his lips are pursed with a sort of question mark. He's thinking. But about what?

CHAPTER EIGHT

Fifteen

It took about a year before our friendship began to falter. Six months into our first year of high school, we had just come back from Winter Break, and our friendship had been the strongest it had ever been. I remember thinking how inseparable we must have been to be able to conquer the transition between middle school to high school.

On the day back, he found me in the commons of our high school cafeteria, where we met since the first week. His hair had grown, even over break, enough so that his curls fell over his forehead in perfect, loose ringlets. His clothes looked all brand new, and once we found a table nearest us, he unzipped his backpack and pulled out a new book.

"Have you read this? My parents just bought it for me," he said, extending his hands towards me with a paperback book, the back facing upright.

"It's called *The Stranger*. I read the entire thing in one day; I think you'd really like it." He shoved the book into my hands, forcing me to take it.

"What's it about?" I asked, turning it over to see the front cover. Its pages looked yellowed and weathered, so I wondered who it lived with before Abe got his hands on it. The cover, also a bit aged, was worn, and the image was faded and a bit tarnished on each corner- as if someone had kept it in their back pocket for safekeeping and it spent years there, rubbing against the fabric of their jeans- displayed a man on a sandy beach. The waves, gentle and frothy, slowly crept up to the man's feet, which lacked any type of shoe, and his face was impossible to read.

"It's about the meaninglessness of life," Abe said finally after swallowing a massive piece of his bagel that he had pulled out of his backpack. Cream cheese hung in a clump on the left side of his lip before his tongue slowly scooped it back up and pulled it into his mouth.

I continued to turn the book in my hands, unsure whether he needed a response or not.

"Thanks, I'll read it," I responded faintly. I wasn't sure why he chose this book to share with me. I almost wondered if, with this book, he was trying to send a message- *you are meaningless, Eli, to me.*

"Bell's about to ring. See you in third?" he said, looking up at the black box with the red digitized numbers on it. I nodded my head, unzipped my backpack, and slid the small paperback into the smallest section, and the bell rang in my ears.

First period, Health, and second period, P.E., were my two least favorite subjects. Not only did I feel utterly unrepresented in both of them, but I also hated the "education" that they provided to us, even then. Looking back now, I know how ignorant my Health teacher had to have been to not teach us about, or refuse to teach us about, healthy LGBTQ+ sex and relationships. But that conversation is for another time and another place.

By the time our third period, American History, rolled around, I felt eager to make it to lunch. Abe greeted me at the door and we walked in together, and I couldn't help but notice that famous Abe smirk on his face as I walked up to him.

"You won't believe it," he whispered to me as I got situated in my seat. Mr. Flannagan knew better than to put us in the same vicinity of the room, so Abe sat up front right by his desk, and I sat in the far back corner- an oversight considering I was the one with glasses who actually needed to see what was being written on the board every day. Abe would also sit beside me until the person who actually sat there got to class or until Flannagan called him to his seat.

"What?" I replied, pulling out the last of my materials for the day.

"You remember Ana from John Henry? She texted me this morning during first. I think now's my shot," he said, the smile still gleaming bright.

My heart sank. Suddenly, I thought back to the book he had given to me before classes started today and how my suspicion must have been true. What does this mean for us?

Ana Sangly, a sophomore at John Henry, used to play in the same soccer scrimmages that Abe played in. She was there that night when I first met him. I knew they were friends, but I never really knew it had extended this far to the point where he actually cared for her this deeply.

"Abe, your seat please" Flannagan said, pulling me out of my thoughts, and pulling Abe farther away from me.

Third period felt like years taken away from me; I completely zoned out from Flannagan's incessant lecture about how the Europeans came over and discovered America (which we all know now is complete and utter bullshit), and watched the clock. The time passed minute by minute like a snail moving across the track towards the finish line. Every time I reminded myself that looking at the clock made time move slower, I always found my eyes gluing themselves back to those red numbers.

Finally, after hours of waiting, the clock turned to that magical number: time to pack up. I quickly and delicately placed my belongings back in my backpack and walked towards the door.

Without even realizing it, I heard the bell ring, and I made a beeline for my car- leaving Abe to wonder where I had gone without him. Once I got to my car, I realized what I had done, so I pulled out my phone.

Sorry, not feeling well. Let me know how it goes! See you tomorrow. I typed into my message box to Abe. *Send.*

Before I knew it, I was back home and regret began to sink it. Everything is going to change, I thought to myself, I'm going to lose my best friend.

I don't know where this thought came from, but I knew that it had to be true. First, Kell, and now Abe. The two people who I truly cared for, who I didn't already have to care for, were gone.

CHAPTER NINE
Border Patrol

As Hudson continued to drive, he spilled his entire life story (without being prompted to, I might add). He mentioned how his childhood seemed altogether dull to him and, now in his late 20s, he wanted adventure. He was basically an only child, and to him, that made his life worse for some reason. His older brother was always an enigma to him, partly because he was never really around but also because even when he was around, he really wasn't. I knew not to pry, and so I didn't. I found it interesting, though, that he didn't mention his age outright or talk much about his parents, and I found myself beginning to wonder why that was. Of course, the thought escaped me almost as quickly as it entered my mind. I couldn't allow myself to care about such things. If not, because they didn't ultimately matter in the magnitude of other things, because they didn't matter to me. I watched him again as he gripped his steering wheel as if it were a close friend. I could tell his car meant a lot to him just by the way he drove it, and I felt compelled to question his morals suddenly.

"So, I know you mentioned the importance of God," I began, and from the back of the car, I could hear Diana beginning to huff, "but what is it that makes Hudson Carver act the way he does?" I finished content with the ambiguity that enveloped my question like a mist. Every question is coated in self-interest, and in asking questions that seem altogether mysterious or open-ended, I feel I am eliminating at least a sliver of that self-interest so that the conversation does not find its way, as it often inevitably does, back to the asker. "Eli, leave him alone already. Didn't he tell you enough about that?" Diana mumbles, shuffling uncomfortably in her seat. Her blond hair has lost its voluminous shine and has, instead, adopted a ratty and almost greasy look. I find myself, in that moment, wondering why we hadn't yet stopped at a hotel and when we would find ourselves at one. The idea of the water coming out of the shower head onto my dirty flesh, washing away the physical memories that have coated us the past few days. If only water had the power to do that to our minds as well as our bodies. Sometimes, no matter how hot the water is or how hard you scrub the soap into your skin, the memories cannot be washed away.

Diana's cough and Hudson's voice jolted me back to reality. Which has more power in doing so, I don't know.

"That is a great question. And one I feel would be best answered second to yours," he says, giving me a side glance while trying to maintain his focus on the road.

"Why is that?"

"Well, why else would you ask me about my morals if it weren't because you were, for some reason, questioning your own?" he said without a second of hesitation. *Dammit*, I think to myself, *how is he so good with these spot-on and speedy remarks.* But then I question his response even more deeply, wondering if he is right. It cannot possibly be true that after thirty-something years, I still do not have a grasp on myself and on the way I and others live our lives and fit into the grand scheme of things. Is that not what morality is all about? Attempting to, in some way, find the purpose that everyone else is searching for before anyone else can achieve it? No one said it would be easy, but why does it have to be a competition?

"I feel pretty content with my understanding of morality and the role that it plays in my life," I reply, after taking a considerable amount of time thinking of the perfect response.

When he doesn't say anything, I continue. "The fact is, Hudson, everyone views morality as a singular thing, right? Singular in that it can either be seen as good or bad, positive or negative, light or dark. Why is that? Because people are too afraid to accept what is right in front of them. Maybe it isn't that a person has to act in a way that labels them as good or bad, that values their life overall as positive or negative, that leaves their existence in light or dark. Maybe it's that there is a middle ground, a grey area. And in that grey area, acceptance that neither of the polar sides of the spectrum of morality actually matter. What if that's the key to understanding a person's morals?"

He took a moment to think. I could tell he was thinking because he tightened and loosened his grip on his steering wheel as if he were using it to suck in some sort of courage or power to speak.

"Well, frankly, I think that you're wrong," he said, "you can't view life without meaning because if there wasn't anything that 'mattered,' we wouldn't exist; simple as that. You would not be sitting in the seat that you are in, and I would not be driving this car. It would not be a sunny day, Diana wouldn't be sitting in the backseat, we wouldn't be having the conversation that we are having right now if none of this mattered," and that was that. I did not want to push the matter any further, not only because I didn't care to hear what else he had to say but because I knew I would hear an earful from Diana when we got out of the car, and the thought of that irritated me. He didn't seem to want to continue the conversation either because, at that moment, he turned the music on and sped the car up just enough for me to notice.

I looked back at Diana, who gave me a motherly look of disapproval, and I almost laughed. I knew that Diana was a mother now, but it didn't suit her at all. Looking back at the front of the car, I continued to watch as cars passed us. At one point, a white minivan carrying a family of five passed us on our left and swerved in front of us unnecessarily. I could see a boy in the backseat window shoving his action figure against the window, either to show it off or to keep it away from his older brother, who was sitting beside him.

CHAPTER TEN

A Pit Stop

We aren't too far from our stop in Dartmouth when Hudson sighs. I look out the window to my right in an attempt to avoid any imminent conversation. Again, he sighs and says, "I think I need to pull over, just for a couple minutes. My eyes are getting tired." I think to respond, but before I have a chance to, he puts the turning signal on and moves over into the right lane, anticipating our exit from the freeway. I take note of the bumps in the road as we slide from lane to lane. Then the thought enters my mind; *is Hudson actually getting tired, or does he simply want to extend his time with us?*

As we exit off the freeway, I notice a sign ahead that says Dartmouth 15 miles. Only 15 more miles, and we will be done with him for good. He takes a right turn from the off-ramp and pulls into the nearest gas station. I roll the window down in an attempt to get some fresh air.

Once he pulls in, he shifts the car into park and turns the car off. I can feel the car sputter out and die without the ignition. The window is still rolled down, which irritates me.

"So, listen, guys. I need to be honest with you," he starts, "I know I told you that there wasn't really much reason for me to be driving in this area, but that wasn't quite the whole truth."

My heart begins to pulse faster, and I can hear it in my ears. Not so much from fear or anxiety, more so from anticipation of what he may say next. It is a strange feeling, and I try to focus on it, but he interrupts again.

"I apologize. I have kind of been running from something…" his voice trails off. It sounds sad, almost nostalgic in a way. His pause makes me feel that he is just trying to wait for a sympathetic response or some sort of pity. Either that or maybe he really is just struggling to try to find the words to say. I turn to look at Diana in the back, and she looks back at me, widening her eyes. I stay silent, deciding that it must just be that he is waiting for a fish to bite his hook, for one of us to speak up and ask for clarity.

"Or, not so much something. Someone," he says, and moves his hands mechanically from the steering wheel down into his lap. It seems forced and inorganic, like someone who is so used to moving through the world gracefully and naturally, as suddenly forgetting all sensibility in expression and no longer functioning well. Not only have his movements changed, but there is more uncertainty and insecurity in his voice than before. The air in the car suddenly turns cold and bitter. The cold must be to blame.

I bite. "What do you mean, someone?" I say, turning my body to face him in the car. My back is now entirely up against the passenger side door, and I feel a gust of wind tickle at the back of my neck. It is small reminders like this that I am human and I am alone.

"My brother. I was supposed to be visiting him on the cape. When I met you two, I was so shocked that you were heading to the same place I kept myself from sharing the whole truth. It's a tricky subject, my brother and I." he looks over towards me. Even though he is looking at me, it feels like he is looking beyond me into the cold air that touches and tickles my back, making my hair stand on end. His expression is emotionless, the lines on his face relaxed, almost as if I am not even here.

"When we were younger, we were best friends. Older brothers, you know, always someone to look up to. But as we grew older, especially once he moved out, it was like he forgot about me. My parents blamed the age gap, 6 years between us. But I lived through my entire high school and most of my middle school experience without someone that I had grown to otherwise know was my one and only support system. That loss is more significant than words can really express."

Hudson reaches back for the steering wheel and grips it tightly.

"That's why I've felt like an only child; I learned I had to be."

I take this opportunity to look in his eyes, to look directly into his eyes and hope to see something more profound. I knew Hudson was a man who felt he mattered, and I found myself, now, finally envying him. How had he been able to experience a loss that seems to have affected him so deeply and still feel such vigor about his life. How could he learn the evil of this world firsthand and still find light? In his eyes, I see something I didn't see before. A different flicker. Pain. It glows almost eerily in his hazel brown irises, little black glowing flecks interrupting an otherwise perfectly simple amber. There was something familiar about that glow.

I'm transported briefly to the year 2015. Standing in the bathroom of the second floor of my grandmother's house, I look into the mirror with my hands on either side of the sink. Pressing against the marbled tiles, the heat from my hand transfers directly into dense slab and I feel a chill shoot through my body. In the doorway, Him. He is leaning against the doorframe, watching me watch myself.

"What?" I say, not taking my eyes off myself in the mirror, trying to find some semblance of who I used to be. He walks up against me and presses his nose into the crease of my neck. I watch it unfold in the mirror like a scene from a movie, like something I always dreamt of but couldn't ever possibly happen to me. But here I was, and the mirror seemed to prove that my dream was a reality.

"Why do you smell so damn good?" he whispers in my ear, and I smile, my eyes glowing with that familiar glow.

Back to the car, only mere miles from Dartmouth, my gaze into Hudson's eyes are interrupted by a man carrying two plastic gas station bags filled with miscellaneous items and a case of beer in his hands saunter back to his pick-up truck.

"I know how you feel," I say without thinking. This is not like me.

"Eli, I am sitting right here," Diana says in a firm but quiet voice. I refuse to look back at her, and I keep my eyes fixed on the space behind Hudson's head.

"I think you needed this trip just as much as we did, Hudson," Diana chooses her words carefully, "and if wherever you plan to meet your brother is close to where our house is, you are welcome to join us if you just need the support of other people" she finishes, and for once I find myself agreeing with my sister's inability to assess a situation appropriately. Or, maybe I realize that, at this moment, it is my inability to assess the situation, and Diana actually has it figured out.

Hudson looks down at his hands, and I can tell that is what he was waiting for. His body begins to tremble slightly. There is something he is not telling us, something that, even now, he has chosen to omit from his declaration.

"I'm with Diana. If it's close to us, I see no reason for you to not join us. If not at the cabin, at least for the rest of the drive. It would be doing us a favor, too."

It was almost on cue that the moment I finished my sentence, he looked up at me. His face drooped lower and, at an angle, passed off a puppy dog look from his eyes. I am half expecting him to say something along the lines of "Do you really mean that?" but instead, he nods solemnly in thanks.

"Do you want me to drive the rest of the way? No need to stop at Dartmouth now, anyways, and we are so close," I say.

"Thank you," he speaks in a muffled and choked voice, clear he is holding back tears. I know he is not thanking me for driving, but for something much more than that.

CHAPTER ELEVEN

Ana Sangly

Ana and I only knew of each other through Abe, though we never formally spent any time together. It's an odd feeling to know so much about someone without ever having met them or spent time with them. When Abe would talk about her, I tended to zone out and focus my mind on other things. She came to our school at the beginning of our Sophomore year. She was a summer baby, apparently, and so she started the second year with her license. Even now, everything he told me about her came flooding back into my head and flipped over and over again like an old movie reel.

It didn't take long for her to infiltrate our time together. First, it was in conversations about her, then it was her beginning to say hi to me in the halls, and finally she became a part of our friendship. It wasn't so clear that she was trying to push me out. To work her way into Abe and I's friendship and completely destroy it. But that is what she did.

It was a Wednesday, I think, and we had a half day. The bell rang at 12:30 to dismiss students, and I thought to walk immediately to the upper lot where my mom always parked, waiting for me. It was my routine, after all, to get food at a drive-thru, go home and work for a bit on my writing, and take a long midweek nap. I was only three months away from getting my license, and I knew it would make things so much easier. I pushed through the crowds of students and exited out the side door by the math wing, where I saw them. They didn't see me at first, and I would have just walked by them without another thought if I weren't so perceptive. They were sitting on the senior steps, a collection of smoothed concrete slabs that sat adjacent to the stairs up to the student parking lot. Adjacent to the stairs up to my car. Ana was dressed in a knee-length pastel floral dress. Her burgundy hair seems to bounce gently against her shoulders as she turns her head and laughs. Abe, on the other hand, is in his standard daily school outfit; a flannel and ripped jeans. Today, he's chosen light blue, perhaps to accent his eyes. The sky, even from this distance, seems to reflect in the whites of his eyes like pools in a vast ocean, and I swear I see a glint in them. As I walk, I become uncomfortably aware of my own feet against the ground. Left, right, left, right. *Is this how I usually walk?* I think to myself. I nearly reach the bottom of the stairs when he sees me.

"Ehhhhhh-liiiiiii!" Abe sings, clutching at his chest with one hand in a dramatic act and his other hand around his mouth to boom his voice even louder than it already was. With as much grace as I can, which overthinking probably means without any, I pivot myself to my left and smile at them. Like I had said, they sat on one of the senior steps, acting like they owned them. He was now standing in front of her, not allowing me to see the expression on her face. Abe sat back down and wrapped his arm around her, and she smiled warmly.

"Hi, Eli! We're going to grab some food. Do you want to come?" I walked closer to them, looking at her briefly before landing my eyes on him.

"No thanks, I figured I would just go home today," I lie. Abe's lip twitched, and I knew he sensed my lie. Only weeks before, my routine was our routine.

"You free this weekend, then?" He said curiously. Ana seemed to give him a look and gently pressed into his ribs. It was so subtle that no one would have noticed it.

"Babe, you know we have that date planned this weekend," she said as quietly as she could without trying to be disrespectful with me standing right there.

I just stood there. It wasn't so much that I was speechless, more so that I just found myself not caring. *Is this where it started?* I look back and wonder. I knew I would care later, though, probably the second I stepped into my car, I would care. But they couldn't know that. I suppose at that moment, I decided that I could not let her win, even though she already had.

He tried to save the moment, "Can't we reschedule that, babe? I haven't really been able to see Eli in weeks." he looked over at me for a moment before lowering his tone, "And it's important to me that you two get to know each other more."

My face began to turn red, and I wanted to interject. I knew he didn't intend for me to hear it, but I did. Why is he putting me in this situation? If I mattered to him, wouldn't he choose me? I couldn't allow that thought to fester because she stood up and hastily slung her backpack around her shoulder.

The sun above us shines harshly against the top of my head. Without a cloud in the sky, it seems even the wind is at a standstill.

Ana shifts on her feet, her curls swaying more to her left side than before. She lifts her backpack, which is more of a tote bag than anything else, and slings it around her right shoulder. It hangs loosely, and I wonder what contents may lie inside. *Could he have given her a book that she is keeping in there? What notes have they sent to each other? What secrets have they told?* She hops down the few large steps to where I am standing and, without saying a word, moves swiftly past me and up the stairs to her car. *If only I had been allowed to leave so easily.* A tinge of guilt washes over me in knowing Ana, and Abe even for that matter, had both received their licenses before me.

I follow her with my eyes until she is out of sight. There seems to be a weight in her step as she ascends the stairs, but I don't dare change the direction of my gaze because I can feel that there are eyes on me. When I finally can't handle it any longer, I turn back to Abe. We make eye contact, and he rolls his eyes at me in an attempt, I believe, to align frustration. But I don't feel any frustration toward Ana. In fact, I feel relief. I feel content in knowing that I had done nothing wrong to cause a reaction from Ana, meaning that it had just been my presence that was an irritant to her. The feeling almost made me smile.

"Will you meet me at our spot?" he says, lifting his own backpack around his shoulders and meeting me at the surface level. I know what he is referring to, but not hearing it after such a long time makes it seem foreign in his mouth now. Our spot is and has been our favorite of the coffee shops we frequent. The one we share with no one else, the one who received the highest rating, and one we have not visited for at least three months now.

"Please," he says, now beside me. I can smell his cologne, the light breeze in the air does nothing to stop the warm glow he emanates. "Please don't let this affect your opinion of her, I mean, she's been stressed and all with work and life" I look at him and his eyes seem to change slightly. There is fear in them, but only for a brief and split second before the warm glow returns.

"No, it's okay. You go," is all I can say, and I feel the imminent human reaction begin to well in me when someone experiences rejection or anything of the sort. It always starts in my gut and travels upward, and then it erupts altogether, freezing my body and my brain in a mix of hot and cold slushy, all like a chemical reaction. I have about a minute left before the tears start to fall. It seems he doesn't even intend to converse for that amount of time.

"Okay," he sighs, "I'll text you tonight, we can figure something out, okay?" he says, and before I even get the chance to respond, even though I have nothing to say anyway, he passes behind me and bolts up the stairs after Ana, skipping steps as he goes. I watch as he goes, as I did with Ana, and I feel a sense of relief.

As I walk up the stairs to my mom, taking careful note to move slowly so as to miss Abe on his way out of the parking lot, my relief turns to paranoia. The thoughts churn from relief to frustration to anger momentarily. Then, from there, to sadness, which shifts directly into embarrassment. *Did I need to fight? Is this my fault? How do I fix this?* I decide as I get in my car to send him a text; it reads, "Hey, let's meet at our spot in thirty. I have something I want to say." The words glow back at me from my smartphone as my thumb wavers over the blue arrow. *Just hit send*, I think, and I move my finger away from the arrow to the words, rubbing against them gently.

Then, my thumb moves over to the backspace, and I watch as the words disappear from my view and from existence altogether.

"Well," I whisper to myself, closing my driver's side door behind me, "maybe I should just wait for him to text me. He said he was going to, after all."

"What?" my mom said, getting in the passenger seat beside me and giving me the chance to practice before my big drive.

"Oh, sorry, nothing" I respond, and turn the key in the ignition, feeling the car hum to life.

CHAPTER TWELVE

Sixteen

"**O**kay and smile in 3…2….1" FLASH. It happened. I was officially licensed, and three days before my big party. Finally, I could tell Abe that I was driving.

I stood in the driver's license office expecting two things: a long line and a celebration after being handed my license in my hand. Unfortunately, neither had happened. I was expecting a line because I had heard all of the horror stories, how it was a sort of rite of passage to attend the DMV because of the line that existed when you entered. Now, the celebration, I understand, was a stretch, seeing as how all government employees don't seem to ever really care about you or anything you are trying to accomplish. However, I was hoping for at least a little enthusiasm when they conducted my eye test and asked me questions about my weight, height, and eye color. If not that, at least a small celebration after the picture was taken.

We walked in about twenty minutes prior, and my mom notified me that she had booked an appointment for us. Upon sitting in the waiting area for no longer than five minutes, a short Asian man approached us and said, "Eli Greene?" in a questioning tone. I rose from my chair and followed him to a corner of the building. It wasn't much bigger than what the floor of a hair salon would be, with four or five open cubicles for employees to conduct their business out of. We walked to the farthest one, and the man took his position behind the desk. The only thing blocking the two of us from each other was a thick piece of plexiglass with an arch carved out for conversation.

He begins by asking for my documents, of which I have prepared already on the counter. One trait I valued so deeply about myself was my ability to be punctual and organized. I handed the paperwork over. He lowers his rounded glasses to the edge of his nose and huffs, seemingly annoyed I was able to present everything he needed with such ease.

Then came the questions: age, height, weight, eye color, hair color.

"Do you want to be an organ donor?" he says plainly.

"What does that mean?" I ask, looking more to my mom for guidance than to him.

"Most people do it; I would just say yes," he responds, and I nod my head. My mom doesn't object, so we move on.

"Alright let's head on over to the sheet over here. Stand on the footprints there on the floor for me please."

I do.

"Okay, and smile in 3…2….1" FLASH. We wait a moment, and the excitement builds in me. "Here you go," he reaches his hand out and hands me two pieces of paper. One is a receipt for sixty-five dollars for the license, and the other is a paper copy of the license with my photo and all the information he had digitally input. "Expect to have the plastic copy mailed to you within the next three to five business days. You are all set to go."

When we make it outside, I go, "That was it?"

"I guess so! I was expecting you to get the real one today. Want to go pick up a few things for your party?" my mom replies, and we step off the curb into the parking lot in unison.

I nod my head as we walk toward the car, feeling like I can't share the news yet with Abe without my plastic license. It wouldn't feel the same.

The next day at school, I couldn't bring my car because I didn't have a parking spot for it yet on the school campus, and my parents didn't want to risk getting a ticket or having it towed. To make it even worse, I had to take the bus because my parents would be out of town until the end of the weekend. While that does mean I get the house to myself without parents, I have to be a licensed teenager still taking the bus to and from school…

When the final bell rang, I chose to linger in the commons. It was the fluorescent lights that appealed to me, made me feel at home for some reason. In the distance I could see a few of my friends, Abigail and Isabel, walking through the halls no doubt in pursuit of getting to their cars.

"Abby! Izzy!" I yell, waving my hand to get their attention.

When they see me, they smile and walk over. Abigail is a shorter girl, somewhat overweight, and she wears her oversized hoodie with a pair of ripped dark blue jeans. Her Converse that she wears every day are scuffed and brown with who knows what. I've always admired her for her eyes; brown, yes, but so full of life.

Izzy, on the other hand, is pencil-thin. She is wearing a pair of ankle-length skinny jeans that are typical all-American blue. Her shirt, tight as well, clutches against her ribs and her small breasts. They are round, perfectly symmetrical, and held up gently by her bra. I watch them as the girls' approach.

"Hey Eli," Izzy says, "are you excited for your birthday party? Is it cool if we come a few hours early? We can help set up still, if you need it."

"Yeah, would you mind? That would be really helpful. Thank you," I respond, looking up into her green and hazel eyes. She is taller than me, not by much, but enough.

She pushes her hair out of her face and behind her ear and Abigail speaks up, "Cool dude, we will be there at 5. You're still getting pizza, right?" I nod my head with a smile.

"What are you doing now? Want to go down to the mall with us?" Isabel says quickly.

"I should probably be getting home, gotta take the bus" I whisper the last part and play it off as a joke, even though I know it isn't.

"Um, no. Come with us to the mall, we will help you get an outfit for Saturday, and then I'll drop you back off at yours after" she responds, matter-of-factly.

I smile again. I appreciated her for not taking no for an answer. Still, I preferred my alone time. But I couldn't pass up on her offer; it was clear, after all, that my presence would be more of a comfort to her than theirs would be to me.

"Alright, but I call backseat middle," I say, knowing there is no point in calling a seat no one ever calls dibs on. Not only that, there were only three of us.

They laugh, and we all walk out of the common floor doors to the student parking lot.

The following two days flew by in a blur. An English essay completed and submitted, a U.S. History presentation choked through, and here we were; the weekend.

The party was in less than four hours, and I lost track of who would be attending. I know Abe would be coming, no doubt bringing his girlfriend. Diana invited a few of her friends too, mainly because of the popularity factor, she said, but I know it was more because she wanted an excuse to throw a party, any chance she got when our parents were away.

From upstairs, I could hear her already getting ready with her friends, their music blaring. We Intended to keep the party on the middle level of the house, blocking off the basement, where my room is, and the upstairs, where our parent's bedroom is. Our home was set up in such a way that gave all of us our own floor, with a bathroom and bedroom, an open area turned into a T.V. room for each of us, and access to the outside, whether it be the backyard, like for me in the basement, or a balcony like for my parents.

My room, on the basement floor, followed a minimalist yet homey theme. A dark brown wooden desk sat in the corner, adorned with my favorite books and laptop. In the center of the room were my personal T.V. and consoles for games, and sitting opposite it, a queen-sized bed with red satin sheets and a white comforter laid symmetrically on top.

It is my bed that I lay on now, waiting for a text from Isabel and Abigail about an update on their arrival. I reach for my phone and send a quick text to Diana asking her when the rest of her friends are coming. After a few minutes, I hear the music turn off and movement from upstairs. It isn't a few seconds later when she comes barging into my room, her friends following closely behind her.

"You ready for tonight?" they all say in unison. I nod my head, trying to feign excitement, but not so well.

"When are your friends getting here with the alcohol?" Diana asks, sitting on the corner of her bed. Her friends, Sabrina and Katie, look up from their phones quizzically, waiting in anticipation for my answer. I was only a year older than Diana, but how did she get so involved in all this stuff so quickly? I only just started drinking with my friends, and I still preferred coffee to alcohol.

"Not sure," I respond, "We still have four hours before it even starts. I'm not worried," I reply, readjusting my head on the pillow so I can lean up slightly.

"Alright, alright. I think Alan is coming with weed for us, too." She replied, turning slightly to face Sabrina.

"Breen, can you text the guys and see if they are still coming?" Sabrina nods.

"No smoking inside, please make sure everyone is aware of that" I respond, reaching again for my phone.

All three girls roll their eyes at me and Diana lifts herself from the bed. They walk out swiftly and as they do; she calls from behind to say "come up in twenty and let's start pregaming!"

It didn't take long for the time to pass and sooner than expected, we were in the middle of the party. Abigail and Isabel had come through with the alcohol tenfold, bringing with them their siblings and their siblings' friends. Our living room, decorated with balloons and streamers, was filled with around thirty people at this point, it was ten o'clock or somewhere around there.

The pulsing music made our drinks go down easier. In my hand was a red solo cup filled almost to the brim with a clear liquid and a single ice cube, almost completely melted. The air was thick and warm with breath and sweat from the bodies moving and standing in place. It didn't take long for the weed rule to be broken- on the coffee table was loose marijuana littered about, no doubt already in the carpet as well. A group of seniors sat on the couch, two girls and a guy, and I walked over to greet them.

"Hey man, thanks for coming!" I say, walking up to the guy first. "I don't think I've met your friends?"

He looks up at me, joint in hand, and takes a long drag. The smoke is held in his mouth for quite some time, and then he turns his head to the girl on his left and blows it into her mouth. A little escapes but is caught by her nose as she strains to breathe in every last strand.

"Dude, Eli, happy birthday!" He says, passing the joint off to the other girl.

"This is Liz Sangly. You may know her younger sister, she's a sophomore. Liz, this is Eli."

Liz looked at me and smiled, and I suddenly recognized the resemblance.

"Hi, Eli!" with enthusiasm in her voice, she rises from the couch and grips me in a tight hug. The alcohol in my system tingles and swirls warmth throughout my entire body, and I hug back tighter.

"It is so nice to meet you, and oh my gosh, happy birthday! Thanks for inviting us." She pulls her head back but keeps her tight grip on me, holding both of my arms now with her hands.

"Of course," I begin, "and you all are welcome to anything in the kitchen. We've got plenty of vodka and fireball. If you want something a little bit better, I have a bottle of tequila in my room. You like tequila?"

"Um, yeah, it's like my favorite!" she responds, turning now to look at Jacob, who is leaning too closely to the other girl. I still don't recognize her, but she is slumped into the couch with her eyes barely open. I make a mental note to make sure to check on her later, or have someone check on her.

"Jacob, Eli has tequila, come on!"

"Do you know when your sister is gonna be here?" I asked, trying not to seem suspicious but also not really caring. She looks back and me, grabs my hand and pulls me along. As we walk towards my room, she says "Oh she probably won't come anymore. She got into some fight with her boyfriend or something. They are always fighting, it's hard to keep up."

I wasn't sure if it was because she was high or just overly honest, but the second she finished speaking, my heart skipped a beat, and I felt my face get hot. The feeling rushed through my body, and it, mixed with the alcohol, opened my vision to a sense where I was suddenly hyper-aware of everything around me.

We passed other people leaning against the wall as we reached the door to the basement stairs. They observed us and the chaos of the party now behind us, torn between wanting to join in with their drinks and socialize or staying on the sidelines. The beat of the party died down the farther we walked from the speakers in the living room, and as I opened the door, my heart sank.

That meant he wasn't coming.

The joy I was feeling seemed to shrink away and melt into the carpet below my feet. I could feel beneath my toes the intricate strands of synthetic fibers tickling my skin; it made my entire body tingle. Liz, who had still been holding my hand, released it and reached for the doorknob. Pulling it open, she looked back to make sure we were both with her, and she descended the stairs.

When we entered my room, I walked straight over to the bottle of Patron, pulled it open, and took a deep pull from the liquid inside. It burned the second it hit my tastebuds, and I wanted to wince, but instead, I kept drinking.

"Shots, shots, shots, shots!" Liz yelled beside me, and Jacob joined in with his half-assed hoots and hollers.

"Okay, okay, give us a chance!" he says, reaching for the bottle. He had to pry it from my hands to get a taste, but I knew the more I drank, the better I would feel. So, I watch him intently, waiting impatiently for another turn.

"To you," he says, holding the bottle up above our heads. We had formed a circle, but I broke it to stand over by my bed, plopping myself down and reaching for my phone.

Three new notifications glow back at me. A text from my mom that reads: Please make sure to take the dog out. Happy Birthday! Another from Diana reads: Do you know who the guy in the grey hoodie and sweats is? Such a loser to show up like that. And the last, the only one that matters, from Abe.

It reads: Hey, Eli! Are you still here?

I look at the time stamp: 10:34 P.M. It was already almost 11:00, how has he been here for twenty minutes and not found me by now? I stand, feeling a bit wobbly, and look at the two still bottle feeding each other from my tequila.

"Let's go back up" I say, reaching for the bottle. Liz and Jacob give each other a small innocent smile and reach over to link arms with me. It is in this way that we walked ourselves back upstairs to the party, music blaring louder than before.

The tone has changed when we reenter. The bodies in the living room have become denser, like sardines packed tightly in their container. The music booms, radiating through the entire house and into my bones. It feels good, the music, as it rushes through me. We walk directly into the center of the dancing, arms still linked, and upon release our limbs begin to flail loosely and my head tilts back in ecstasy. This feels good.

I almost forgot to look around, remembering my true purpose for wanting to return back to the party. My mind feels clouded as if I would have to trudge through thick clouds to reach any rational thought.

Someone taps me on the back and I spin my body. Just like my mind, my body is densely populated with the thick clouds that make it more difficult to move. Smoke now fills the airs, the smell of alcohol more intoxicating than ever. He leans in close to my ear and yells over the music, "Finally found you!" It was Abe.

I wrap him in a hug. Annoyed, yes. Confused, yes. Still happy? Yes.

"I've been looking everywhere for you," he says, louder now. I turn to walk towards the outside circle of dancing in the hope to hear him more clearly. He grabs my hand and pulls me in the other direction, though, toward the deck. He opens one of the glass French doors outward towards the deck and a gust of cold yet refreshing air meets us.

I step outside with him and almost immediately feel the cold wash over me, and it revives me and gives me a rush throughout my entire body.

Our deck is a self-standing one, with no stairs down to the backyard. With a glass floor and glass railing, it shows off its sleek design more clearly at night with the moon reflecting against it, leaving little sparkles of light on the grass below. There are multiple seating areas, but we walk over to the corner with the bar, loveseat, and firepit.

From this end, no one inside could see us unless they were in Diana's room, which also had a pair of French doors out to the deck. The lights from her room are on, but the curtains are closed and it doesn't seem like there is anyone inside. Abe sits, drink in hand, on the single chair next to the loveseat.

Before sitting, I look out at the skyline. The city, which is clearly in view from this angle of the deck, unfolds before me, a living, breathing entity that never ceases to amaze me. The distant hum of traffic, even at this hour, with flickering lights from the skyscrapers and the occasional sirens, create a symphony of the urban world. No matter how many times I've stood here, the view never grows old. It's a constant reminder of the beauty of the world, of the magnificent opportunities and possibilities awaiting me in my future. Each day, I am grateful for this little corner of paradise, my glass deck overlooking the city, a treasure that I genuinely cherish with all of my heart. He is watching me intently, so I sit, crossing my legs against the edge of the loveseat and leaning my body into it toward him.

I feel an overwhelming sense of strangeness wash over me like this moment was lived before by someone some time ago. It's a familiar feeling, one that pulls back memories of my childhood. Was it nostalgia for what once was or something much darker?

"Happy Birthday, Eli" he says, lifting his cup. I want to ask him why he is here, alone, but I can't seem to find the words to ask. So, I just lift my cup to his and smile.

The air around us had changed; I couldn't pinpoint why that was. He smiled back before looking out to the black sky, polluted so much so that no stars were visible. But they had to still be there. I thought to pull out my phone and send a text to Abigail or Isabel, letting them know where

I was and asking them where they were. I decided against it. We were back, the two of us, and I didn't want to miss out on the fleeting moment that this might very well be. Instead, I quickly put on my favorite playlist, and the music begins to play gently from my phone's speakers.

I finally work up the courage to ask, "Where is Ana?" I can't look at him, but I know he is eyeing me now. Instead, I look to the sky, trying to find where it was he was looking just seconds ago.

"She didn't want to come." he said, sighing, "well actually..." he continues, slouching forward toward me.

"I just didn't really want her to come." A pause. The space between us seemed to close, the air standing flat around us, even the wind had taken note and stopped its movements.

I thought to ask him why, but he didn't give me a chance, "I miss this," he said, moving on. He pushes my leg with his knee, and I can't help but feel a shock of warmth run through my leg and up into my stomach.

"I miss us, Eli."

My body starts to shiver, whether from the cold evening air or from his words, I don't know. We were miles from the water and yet I could still feel its pull.

"Me too," I want to say more, but he looks up again toward the sky.

"I don't know what happened to me this year. I got too distracted by the excitement of having a girlfriend. I don't even know if I want a girlfriend." He lifts one of his hands from his leg and runs it through his hair. I watch as each hair moves delicately through his fingers and then lays back in the exact position it was in prior.

He continues, "Well, it won't matter what I want after tonight anyway. Ana and I got into a fight tonight," he says, pausing. I can tell there is more he wants to say, but he doesn't.

"I'm sorry to hear that," I say, frustration rising in me slightly because this is not the type of conversation I want to have with Abe, let alone a conversation I want to have with him on my birthday of all days. But the frustration passes and excitement replaces it as I realize what this really means, the gravity of what he is telling me.

"Maybe we can talk about it tomorrow over coffee?" I say, looking at his face. His gaze is still on his legs, unlike him during conversation, and I will him to look at me with my eyes. After a few moments, he does, and I can see tears have begun to fill his eyes.

"I can't lose this again, Eli. I can't lose you again."

"If that's true, then do something about it." I meant it more as a playful jab, but I could tell he was hurt by it. He closes his eyes tightly, pushing the last remaining tears to fall from his lashes down his face.

He reaches, with his eyes still closed, for my hands. I begin now to realize why the air has changed; it wasn't so much the air but us. He has my hands in his and the temperature of his skin awakens my senses.

"I plan to," he says plainly and leans forward toward me.

I've only been river rafting once in my life. It wasn't something I wanted to do, but I did it anyway. It was a beautiful day and we had driven a long way to reach the starting point of the river, a calm point that pushed the flow of water gently but with fluidity. I knew I would enjoy getting out on the water, feeling the rush of having to push through a wave or over a small waterfall. The excitement in my friends' eyes as our instructor doubled down and told us to expect a challenging run. But the fear of the unknown is more powerful than the unknown itself. Sometimes, the unknown isn't even an unknown if you don't know it as a possibility to be unknown. River rafting was an unknown I knew. I could identify exactly what I didn't know about it, and for that reason, it developed a fear inside me.

But this kiss was not even an unknown I thought was an unknown. And so, when Abe's lips, now cold from the evening air and from his nerves, found their way onto mine, I felt no fear. Our lips pushed against one another in perfect harmony, like they were made to match, and we held like that for a few moments. I could feel his lip begin to quiver, and he pulled away, but only for a moment, before smashing his lips against mine again, this time harder and with more force. I followed his lead, pursing my lips and squeezing his hands, feeling his warmth and my warmth became one, synced in every way.

His tongue pushed through my lips, entering my mouth gently and with hesitation. I could feel, as our lips continued to work, his tongue discovered every inch of the front of my teeth. It fought for a passageway further, and so I opened my mouth, and our tongues began a dance with each other, a dance that only they knew and was theirs alone. No one would be able to take it from them; no one would be able to witness what they were capable of.

Our lips, along with our skin, were now both warm to the touch. It felt good to know that we were offering each other this pleasure. I allowed my mind to give in entirely, the kisses becoming more and more blurry, my thoughts blending with the alcohol and into his lips. I pushed my tongue back against his and entered his mouth, where the dance continued with more vigor this time. I pulled back gently, bringing my own tongue back into my mouth, and he followed with his own. I sucked gently, pulling his into my mouth as our lips locked into place.

This unknown was one I didn't even acknowledge as an unknown. Here I was, experiencing it and feeling…. good. More than good. My body shivers, now with anticipation, and my mind wanders for a moment back to the fear I felt while stepping into the raft before being pushed out into the center of the moving river. Fear and whatever this feeling was that I was experiencing now felt the exact same, except one felt good.

The song changed abruptly and a piano began to play, slow at first, and then starting to pick up speed. The beautifully gentle, strained, and one-of-a-kind voice from Patrick Watson fills the air in exact accordance with the tone of the moment.

"Hey, um Eli?" It was Abigail. I quickly pulled away and looked at my friend. My eyes strained to see her as she had come from Diana's room, her lights that had remained on illuminated this entire half of the deck. Behind her was my sister.

"Abigail! I was going to text you; where did you go?" I say, wiping my mouth with the back of my hand.

"Sorry, I had to call Isabel an Uber. I was gonna ask, is it cool if I crash with you tonight?"

I nod my head, "Of course, don't even think about it. Let's go get another drink! Abe, you wanna join us?" I say, looking back at him. His eyes were soft, and he had a slight smile on his face. It made me feel good to know that regardless of what Abigail had just seen, what had just happened was ours and ours alone. And he knew that.

"Oh, and Abe, Ana called me and asked where you were," Abigail says, "I think she might be on her way here or already here." Just then, Diana turns, and behind her, I see Ana walking through her bedroom door with her sister, Liz, and Jacob. They all join us on the deck. I reach for my phone, turning the music off at once.

Abe stands and walks over to Ana. Our moment was lost just then, and that familiar feeling of fear replaced the unfamiliar feeling of our kiss.

"Eli, let's go get another drink," Diana says, waving her hand towards her room. She knows, I think to myself, and I feel grateful for that.

CHAPTER THIRTEEN

A Lie

The events from my party lived and died in the alcoholic haze that covered the night in a rose-colored film. When I woke up the following morning, I received a text from Abe that said: Sorry about last night, I didn't expect it to go the way it did. I'm still here for you if you ever need it.

My head was fuzzy but it did not hurt, although I felt exhausted. I pushed the phone beneath my pillow and decided to sleep again. It happened quickly, when the sleep came, as dreams started flipping across the blackness of the void that was created from the absence of lights when my eyes closed.

First, I was in the pews of my church again, but it wasn't me whose body I had entered. It was almost as if I was a purveyor of my own future, but I knew it couldn't be real; Kell stood at the altar of the church. Beside her was another woman, both of them dressed in beautiful white gowns that cascaded over the ugly carpeted steps, making it seem as though they were walking on a white carpet.

The light from the stained-glass ceiling shone brightly, with an almost iridescent and ephemeral glow across everyone and everything in the room. I looked around to see the smiles of the people sitting in the pews, every aisle lined entirely from end to end with bodies. I scanned the crowd for any familiar face and found my own, towards the back. I looked the same age as I was now, but surrounded by everyone else, I looked older. My eyes were drooped, tears swelling in them. My face looked gray and dull like I had been avoiding the sun or the outdoors altogether. I was wearing a button-up white T-shirt with black pants and brown leather shoes. My knees bounced up and down from behind the pew, reverberating a small but repetitive clicking sound across the floor, muffled only by the thick wood of the seat. I had never seen myself like this, never before in a dream and never before, with such sadness on my face. I looked back at Kell, who was crying now, too; a smile widened on her face as the man between the two of them announced the completion of their wedding ceremony. Everyone stood, and a mist enveloped all of them. Then, suddenly, everything went black.

I was somewhere new now but not altogether unfamiliar. It was a beach, one I knew I had been to before, perhaps at a place farther down the beach that I had never walked to or explored yet. I saw up ahead where the beach curved into a tall rock bed. Large boulders, some jagged and others smooth, lined that end of the beach. Up above, a cliff, with tall green fir trees swaying slowly in the wind.

The waves were calm, unmoving almost, and there was someone else on the beach. It looked to be a woman much older than me, and she walked toward me at a steady pace. Fog began to come in from the side of the rocks, out toward the water and it was a weird sight to see; fog and water at odds with each other, fighting to have space to push on and to push forward. She defied both and walked her own path, but she was not getting closer. I was in my body again, and I looked down at my own feet. I was bare feet, my toes now completely sunk in the damp sand. I didn't bother to work my way out.

The person stopped, and I saw her more clearly. She had darkened skin and long, flowing black hair, and her eyes looked shaded or veiled somehow. She was not smiling, but she did not seem angry. She had a look of determination on her face. I thought to call out to her, but when I tried my voice did not work. She turned and walked toward the water further and further until all that was left of her was the top of her head, bobbing against the calm waves of the ocean. I could feel tears falling from my face, the wind picking them up and chilling them more than the sight I just witnessed.

When I awoke again, my face was wet. Diana stood over me. She sat on my bed, and I could feel the sheets tighten against my skin.

"Did you have fun last night?" she said, and I wiped the tears from my face.

"Yeah, you?" I sat up in my bed.

She nodded slowly, scratching her forehead.

"Do you want to talk about it?" I knew what she was asking about, and I still didn't want to put too much thought into it, so I shook my head. It took her a moment, but finally, she stood and walked out of my room.

In the weeks that followed, Abe and Ana's relationship grew stronger somehow, and I saw less and less of him. It wasn't until the end of the year that I knew it was over, that his presence in my life had all but been erased and everything leading up to that point had been meaningless. Or, perhaps not meaningless, but an absolute and complete lie. Perhaps those were the same thing.

CHAPTER FOURTEEN

Seventeen

Lou died on the sixteenth of August, three months after my sixteenth birthday. He existed in the world to me as one of those people who seem to have perpetually existed as an elderly person, never having a childhood or a past.

From what I had heard, he worked on the railroad since he was young. He had a fascination with it, and with trains. When his wife died, even before I was born, he sold his home and moved into a one-story rambler in a coastal town only two miles from the beach.

He was our neighbor, one of the full-time residents of the cape, and it quickly became a highlight of our year to be able to drive out to our vacation home and see him.

It started small. Our parents were talking to him one day while they were driving by, and he was outside in his driveway getting the mail. He had told them about his passion and trains and had gotten excited when they told him they had two children of their own. From there, we slowly evolved into being his second family. His own children, now grown with families of their own, had all but forgotten about him. They lived in different states across the country, and since he wasn't up to travel so much anymore, he never saw them. He began scheduling doctors' appointments around the time we were in town so we could take him, always asking when we would come over to see the new tracks he had built for his trains to run on.

We even started going to the vacation home more often for him. We would go maybe once or twice more every year to watch him, his face bright and warm, as he showed us his new track. The trains, vintage and entirely metal, would chug on through every room of the house, going up long hills and falling down with pristine control across furniture, light fixtures, and under beds that were like tunnels lit only by the passenger car lights inside the train. We would follow it around the house like a train ourselves, single file all throughout the different rooms, feeling as though we were entering a new world every time.

It didn't quite occur to me how special of a moment it was for him as it was for me and Diana. I can picture him now, imagining him while we are not there preparing his next build. Or, perhaps, simply finding his place in his comfy chair. After years of use, it had conformed to his form and his form only. T.V. on, T.V. dinner from the microwave on his makeshift table, enjoying his solace each evening. The monotony of this hoping and waiting for the day when we arrived back in town to see the trains.

The fascination for me died not out of distaste or any malintent toward him but simply through the process of growing up and moving on. It wasn't until maybe twelve or thirteen, I had held on as long as I could because I started to take pity on the old man. Lou, once a God in my mind, had just become a man with a bunch of toy train tracks in his home.

And so, years after, when news of his death had come from the cape, I didn't give it much thought besides *who was with him in his last moments beside his trains?*

It didn't hit me until my birthday that not only had I lost him, but I had also lost most of my memory of him. Now, looking back, of course, that is the cycle of life. What is created in life, what is valued and appreciated, dies, and the world moves on.

CHAPTER FIFTEEN

The Rose

Reflections of the past are nothing more than resurfacing the most painful moments of one's life for no reason other than to attempt to feel again. Lou had died, and the rose lady followed soon after. Again, as a kid, the impact was minimal. The normal sentiments "Oh, that's sad" or "I can't believe that" were made, of course, to fulfill the adult need to make it seem like they actually cared. But life moved on without her as it always would.

I knew her as the rose lady. She was up at six in the morning and didn't leave her garden until seven at night. Watering, caring for her flowers, grooming the lawn, and making sure no one stepped foot on the grass. She had lost her husband years before, those in the neighborhood who knew her well enough joked that her garden was her husband's replacement.

It wasn't just her intense dedication to her lawn that always made me fear her. It was the dogs she had tamed to patrol the perimeter of the grass. They were genetically engineered, it seemed, not to leave excrement on her lawn and to bark at anyone who came too close; God forbid they were to accidentally step foot on the perfectly manicured blades of grass that only she and they were allowed to lay their toes upon. But it wasn't the grass or the trees or the shrubs that gave her the name in the neighborhood. It was her roses, nationally recognized and awarded for their beauty. In the front was a perfectly selected row of roses that followed the outline and curves of the perimeter of the yard. In the back, rows and rows of multicolored roses of different genera and sizes were lined perfectly parallel to each other. In between each row is a thin strip of grass with only enough room for one person to walk through. The roses were protected by a barbed wire to keep away pests and critters.

To align with the manicured garden, the dogs stayed manicured as well. They were completely white, whiter than snow itself, and were always kept that way. The dogs and her lawn, her only two loves, and the only two things I knew about her that she loved.

If anyone were playing a game in the street and a ball or toy was thrown onto her lawn, there was no getting it back. Everyone knew to not even think about it, not even try to devise a plan to get the toy back. It was gone, lost to the jungle of her lawn.

The dogs, which started as four of them, were an extension of her life force. It was only when they died that she grew weaker, that she looked visibly older. But still, she was out in the grass every day from dusk till dawn with the dogs that remained, and the lawn was unchanging in its beauty. Almost like the secret garden, a secret not because we didn't know where it was but because it always remained a mystery as to how it stayed so perfectly beautiful throughout the seasons.

When the final dog had died, we knew it wasn't going to be soon after that she would follow them. I always wondered what would happen to the garden.

When she died, our curiosity got the best of us, and when her lawyers decided to make an estate sale for her home, we attended.

The story of her life unfolded then, only after she had died, for me. Stepping into her home, for the first time in my short life, I was affronted by the smell of mildew and mold. It was a familiar smell, though I couldn't place it. My father and I walked through the entryway and into the living room. Outdated carpet covered the floor, and stains in places were covered thoughtfully with blankets and towels that held all of her possessions. Pots, pans, trinkets, and everything else that a person collects in their long life, only to become someone else's property or thrown into a dumpster somewhere to be buried in the earth along with the body of its last owner.

I followed quietly, the house an eerie quiet even though it was filled with people. We all knew there was something odd about this, standing in a deceased person's home looking at their belongings, things that they had spent time, money, and effort to cultivate in a way that brought comfort to them, only to be hastily thrown out and bartered for a buck. We smiled softly at each other as we passed by, taking account of each item and creating a story for it as we passed.

"I didn't know she had kids," I said, passing by a barrage of frames on the floor still filled with family pictures. The wall behind the place they lay had been marked of their previous location, perfectly stained rectangles littered across the floor in disarray. A sign of a home well lived in, or a sign of lack of care?

My dad nodded, looking at the pictures with genuine sadness. "I grew up with them," he said, "they stopped visiting after their dad died. I don't know where they are today." I felt I owed it to her, and now to my father, to look a bit longer. I thought to myself, *how long had she lived here?* The familiar feeling surfaced from my stomach and up into my throat, almost choking me with anxiety: *she had lived a life before me;* what could it have been?

I turned slowly, still trying to maintain an aura of respect about me, being hyper-aware of my words, movements, and expressions. Facing me now was her bookshelf. It was two bookshelves, actually, side by side. They were floor-to-ceiling, a facet of the wall rather than a purchased piece of furniture placed there. Made of dark walnut, the two of them stood tall and heavy, giving home and refuge to hundreds of titles. I immediately recognized many of them- I had read them in school.

"Why did she have so many books?" I said, walking toward them, reaching for one on the third row.

"She was a high school English teacher." my father said, reaching for one himself. "She lent me this copy when I was a kid" he showed me the front cover, *Adventures of Huckleberry Finn*. I smiled, "you should get it" I said, reaching for a few more.

She was an English teacher in a past life. Before her lawn, before her dogs, she had been what I always dreamed to be. And this is what her life had amounted to? An almost seventeen-year-old rummaging through her old belongings.

"What are you thinking about?" my dad said just then. My arms were filled now with twenty titles, duplicates of some even.

"Oh, nothing. Can I get these?" I said, looking down at the books, afraid now to make eye contact in case he somehow had read my mind and knew what I had been thinking about.

"You think too much. Yeah, let's go," he said, walking toward the kitchen table that had been turned into a makeshift cashier stand. My face flushed with embarrassment, and I followed him, sifting through my newfound treasure. I thanked her quietly for the gift. I felt it only fitting that I honor her in some way, feeling that by keeping these books in my possession, I was able to keep her alive somehow.

The woman sitting at the kitchen table looked up at me and smiled from her seat. "Found some good ones?" she said. I knew she was just trying to make small talk, but I winced at her words.

"Yeah, I think so," I responded shyly, clutching them tighter against my chest.

"How many do you have?" I counted quickly and told her. "Does 5 dollars sound okay to you?" she looked at me, after doing some calculations on her notepad. My eyes widened and I looked at my dad. Each one of these books would've been worth at least ten, if not more, and I was getting all of them for five dollars? I wanted to rebut but knew better than to do that. She didn't care.

My dad handed her a five, and we left.

We walked home, across the street, and I went straight to my room to purview my new treasure. I didn't expect it, but tears began to fall. *You think too much.* It had stuck with me. It wasn't an understanding of what I was thinking but rather that my act of thinking at all was wrong or inappropriate. I thought about it, about how I essentially wasn't allowed to feel good about my ability to feel.

I tucked each book away into its new home in my bookshelves and sat on my bed, taking a few more moments just to look at them. The smell of the home lingered on the books and into my room, infecting the others in my collection. The scent had even enveloped the room in its entirety, and I felt comforted.

A few months had passed after that, and the news had been announced. Her house was to be torn down and, in its place, a brand-new triple-level home. The secret garden, now to be buried along with the rose lady, the dogs, and the home, would remain only in the minds and memories of her neighbors. What a burden, I think, to have to carry. Because when we are to die, not only is it us that dies, but it is the memories of her that die with us. Then, she is truly nothing to the world. The most beautiful garden in the world, manicured daily by a single person, was gone and had been wiped from the earth. And there was no one left to care.

III.

THE MIDDLE

NOWHERE TO LOVE

CHAPTER ONE

Amar ch'a nullo amato amar perdona

Everyone can name one person that they have loved and will always love. If they cannot name one person, they haven't felt it yet. It will happen, of course, and it will hurt. Dante spoke cryptically about love, but how else can one talk about such an obscure thing. Something that no one can touch, but everyone knows. Love is divided and breaks off into as many different subsets and as many different meanings as one person wants it to. For these purposes, I am not discussing the love that we feel for our parents or the love that we feel for our friends. I'm not discussing the lack of love that we may feel from these two, but rather the love that we feel for one person. Singular. This love is unlike any other love and is unmatched in its power. We don't know why, and it may forever remain a mystery in the nature of humans, but we all know that there is a love that exists immensely in one other person. For my father, it is my mother. Her beauty, her compassion towards everyone she encounters, and her existence are things that my father fell in love with—an existence unmatched by any other woman in his life. For my mother, it was Gonzalo. A love lost to her, a love that got away. When she first told me about him, I saw her eyes light up, and I wondered why. Looking back, after having met my one love, I pieced it all together.

She was on a trip abroad, somewhere very close to Paris, and she was studying for her thesis. My mother's intelligence is my favorite thing about her; it birthed the need for knowledge within my own soul. Almost a desperate need to understand everything about life; her stories as a young woman motivated me to never lose that unquenchable thirst for information. She lost it, I assume, shortly after Gonzalo or perhaps upon meeting my father, but every now and again, I see glimpses of it.

So, the story begins somewhere very close to Paris. She was out enjoying her youth at a café sometime midday. I imagine the sun shining brightly down on my mother's beautiful brown hair, illuminating the red undertones. Her friend, who I'll call M because I can't quite remember it, was with her, enjoying the sun and the view. My mother, however, was focused on her literature. Two young women, one sun-tanning in the summer sun of Paris, the other with her nose stuck in her book, both with their uneaten strawberry scones atop shining porcelain. M was blond, my mother had told me, and she was a very thin girl. I've only seen one photo of the two of them. It was black and white, though their smiles gave a hint that Paris and everything that existed within it had, somewhere, the life that they were meant to live. Gonzalo was my mother's waiter, and the story seems to start and end there. They fell in love that summer and no number of details would do the love between them any justice, so I have to leave it as is. M moved her way through Paris and found her life. Although I don't know if M found love, I know that my mother did. But she had obligations at home, and she couldn't risk everything to be with Gonzalo in a country that she had only learned everything about from the novels she had buried herself in. So, she left him. She had to. We all have to.

My love didn't find me in another country but rather right at home, in New York. I loved Kell, but she wasn't my love. My love came to me like a tornado. I was wrapped up in a love I never expected to experience with a person I would have never expected to be with; a man. Men and women alike have changed my soul, some for the better and some for the worse, but no one has changed me the way that he did. He, like Gonzalo, is lost to me. If there is one thing I would warrant humans as finding meaning in their lives, it is through love. In love, humans are blinded by the chaos of inferno and can, for that reason, live happily and with purpose. Some of us, like my mother and myself, are unlucky, and we have that right stripped away from us.

I was twenty.

CHAPTER TWO

Fairhaven

Only forty minutes now to the cabin, we had settled into a more fluid routine. Hudson was the navigator, a role that was unnecessary but made him feel important. Diana was on music, and her choices were somewhat fascinating to hear. And me, the driver. Forty minutes away meant we were going to make it just as the sun set below the skyline, falling away from the earth and leaving us no trace of light except that from the light glow of the moon. That, of course, and all of our technology.

We haven't talked much since pulling over to the gas station, and I feel grateful for that. However, I know Hudson feels embarrassed. It is a feeling that still lingers in the air and seems to poke at me any chance it can. Along with that, he has been watching me, and I'm sure he is making minute observations about the type of person I am or must be. But his attempt fails, as I see him in the corner of my eye.

Driving again outside of the city, I started to feel a flicker of enjoyment. The passing sun left short waves of heat against my face as I went, and I began to wonder if I was chasing something. Something other than the sun. A foolish thought.

"I have always wondered," Hudson began, "if the city is just not meant for me anymore." There he goes again, somehow anticipating my thoughts and giving them life by speaking them into existence. Mine stay trapped as thoughts, swirling, not leading anywhere.

"Do you ever think maybe we have made a mistake, advancing so much as a society? I mean, look at the stars," he points up, and I follow his finger. The sky, now quickly fading from blue to orange to black all before my eyes, pulls aside its veil to reveal the sparkling dots that will inevitably litter the sky. *Are they always there?* I think, *even during the day?*

"I never see stars when I'm in the city; it's so easy to forget that they're even there." He crouches lower in his seat to get a better view from the moon roof.

"All this light and tech, building cities on cities. Erasing the past with every new advancement. Bigger and better is the goal, but since when is human complicity better?"

"What do you mean, complicity?" Diana says in the back. I look at her through the rearview mirror and see her hands are between her legs, holding each other tightly. Diana has never shown so much interest in conversations like these.

"Well, think about it. We have all this potential as humans. We have so much ability to learn and adapt, and I mean, we have done a great job at adapting to things that make it easier for us not to think. But what if we had just gone in a different direction, you know?"

I knew what he meant, but I had never had words to put to the feeling. Intelligence in this form is futile in today's world, so it's best to just push it away and continue living. But in continuing to live, it could be true that I have allowed myself to become complicit in it as well. So, how do I break that feeling then? Is that what will finally revive me and bring me back to that moment before…. Him? Was it Him that caused this travesty within my mind that turned it from a universe to a multi-thought fleeting abyss? Or could it have been something bigger, something more sinister that, as time passed, snuck its way into every facet of my mind and rotted it, replacing it even with a thoughtless cog?

Diana must have said something because Hudson continued.

"It's all a matter of importance. What is important anymore, anyway? Eli, what is it that allows you the feeling that all but transcends others? What is it that gives you euphoria?"

I wince at his word choice and grip the wheel a bit tighter. *Who talks like this?* I think.

"Nothing," I start, and before realizing it, I say "anymore..." under my breath.

"What do you mean anymore? C'mon, that can't be true; there must be something. There is always something. Even if it's just something you feel you've lost, what was it?"

I've had enough. He can't just continue speaking to me as if I have to tell him everything about myself, about my life. I will myself not to respond, not to speak, and instead to stare ahead at the asphalt, darkening from its disturbingly gray tone to a darker black. What only ten minutes ago was a brand-new strip of road is now becoming a river transporting my darkest thoughts in silence.

"My work is one thing that I have always loved," Diana saves me from drowning. "I think I'd like to go back to it someday. Or, at the very least, find something in place of it."

"There you go! That is something!" Hudson says, turning from me and looking back at Diana. He has repositioned his body away from me, even, maybe, to signal that I have finally broken his desperate attempt to learn about me.

"What is it about your work that you love so much?" he asks.

"The creativity of it. I was able to let my mind spark in a million different directions and create art in a way that I could be proud of. I think if I were to do it again, I would like to create my own studio. Bring people in, teach them my skills, and allow them to benefit..." she pauses for a moment. It's funny how the people in a space can drive the way the air feels. Now, it feels almost hopeful.

"I would really like that." I can tell she must be crying by the way her voice wavers towards the end, and I think that it may even be real rather than just for show.

"That's really beautiful, and I hope you can get back to something like that, Diana," Hudson responds, reaching his hand back to her.

"For me, it is my stories and the stories of others. Boy, my brother used to tell the most amazing stories. He had always dreamed of being a professor like you, Eli. I don't know what happened. I still want to look up to him and, like I told you both before, even have a relationship with him. I just don't know how anymore. It's like any relationship we did have is gone, and the feelings have been taken with it."

A long pause. The sun, now finally taking its bow across the horizon, winks at us delicately. We are almost there. I think to speak, but right as I do, my phone rings and I realize it is still in the passenger seat cupholder. Hudson grabbed it and, without thinking, slid his thumb across the bottom of the screen. He looked over at me apologetically but put the phone on speaker.

"Hello?" I said, waiting in angst to hear a familiar voice respond.

"Hey, Eli! It's Greg, Greg Lillian? Hey, I just wanted to give you a call, you got a second?" his voice came through clearly through the sound waves.

I waited, "Oh, yeah, hey Greg, what's up?" I replied, embarrassment starting to creep slightly under my skin.

"I wanted to check in with you about something. You know, you're up for tenure here in the department, and I figured we could get a head start on your proposal to the board," he pauses. I look over at Hudson. He smiles at me.

"So, listen, when you are all done with your little road trip," I hear a slight huff from the other end of the line, and Diana, behind me, whispers, "What the hell is that supposed to mean?"

"Maybe we can set up a time to work on it together, say over dinner and a couple bottles of wine?" I roll my eyes but immediately regret it, knowing that Hudson is eyeing me closely.

Greg, again, is an amicable guy. He does his job adequately and I have no reason, now, to decline him.

"Yeah, Greg, that sounds great," I respond with as much enthusiasm as I can. It wasn't so much that I cared to work with him; I just knew he still had power, and that was no reason to hold a vendetta or grudge over him.

"Great, well give me a call when you get back home. I will send over some details tonight so you can have some materials prepared" he says, "oh and Eli, before I let you go, I'd be remiss if I didn't ask- how is your sister and her new kid?"

"Greg, I'm sorry now is actually not a great time. Can I give you a call back later?" I say, hanging up the phone before he can respond. I will deal with the repercussions later. Not so much that there would be any, but more so the fact that hanging up on your boss for whatever reason is probably not encouraged or recommended.

"What did you do that for?" Diana said behind me.

"It was starting to get a bit weird," Hudson said in a muffled tone, putting the phone back in its cup holder. I continue driving.

Thirty more minutes.

"Hey Eli, do you remember this song?" on the radio, the sound projects from each of the speakers, and that song fills the air of the car.

The piano starts gently at first and then builds with that familiar soft voice. It is interesting to hear it again, but now I feel nothing except regret. The physical pain had passed, replaced by one that was actually real and then destroyed altogether. Still, I wonder why it is this song Diana chose to play.

CHAPTER THREE

The Coffee Shop

It happened in a coffee shop. His eyes were on me, and my peripheral vision caught on almost instantly. My eyes at the time, however, were on the barista, who moments ago had taken my order and smiled at me for a little too long. You know that kind of smile that someone gives when they want you to make a move? Yeah, that kind of smile. And so, I was watching as the barista made my coffee, and a tang of frustration began to rise in me. *What is he doing, looking at me like that?* I thought to myself, *is that look even something to* get hung up on?

"Iced Soy Latte for Eli" the barista called, taking me away from my thoughts. I quickly stepped towards the bar and grabbed my iced coffee. I glanced at the name tag pinned sturdily to his apron and I smile at the name; Robin. Before turning back and walking to my seat in the café, I make sure to look him in the eyes with my smile.

I sit down on the couch that's tucked into the corner. It's my favorite spot to be, far in the back corner where no one can observe me but I can observe everyone. The wall behind me displays art from local painters who are hoping to sell their work. The couch, though old, allows for just enough cushion to sit upright on and get work done. Not only that, it's not technically meant for one person, but I had never had a problem up until today.

"Hi, do you mind if I sit here?" I hear through my headphones. *Dammit, I should have left after getting my coffee*, I scold myself. But I came here to write my essay for English 201, and so I had to stay, or else it wouldn't be getting done. Turning my gaze slowly, I made direct eye contact with him. Hazel eyes, dark brown hair, and a gorgeous smile look down at me. He who was looking at me while I was looking at the barista. He whom I should have been asking what the complexities of a smile were. He would change me forever.

"Of course," I said, motioning to the chair beside me. Glancing around the establishment, I notice that besides us, there is only one other couple sitting at a table by the door.

"Thank you," he sighs in relief, removing the satchel he has strapped around his chest and taking a seat next to me. He is wearing brown boots and a solid white tee covered by a dark brown and black flannel. His dark grey chinos are tight around his small but toned calves. I observe, out of the corner of my eye, as he sits down at the opposite end of the couch and uses the space between us to unload all of his materials; a laptop adorned with stickers, a notebook, his phone, and a cup of yogurt with a spoon. I can't help but notice a similar leather string hiding ominously from underneath his shirt. Between the hem of his shirt and the veins on his neck, a sterling silver chain glitters beneath the leather string. I pull my own laptop closer to me and unknowingly begin to finger the stickers I have placed on the outer side of the screen. My fingers find one in the top right corner that is one-half of an Ernest Hemingway quote. It reads "write drunk," and I'm sure you can deduce what the other half might say. It was something I shared with a classmate of mine, and I giggle at the thought, me- the writer, her- the editor.

"Are you in the English program by any chance? What year are you?" he says, glancing over at my open essay.

"This is my second year," I say, "I'm currently writing about one of James Joyce's short stories."

His eyes light up, and I instinctively look down.

"Dubliners?" he says, and upon naming the title of the selection of short stories I'm working on, I look back up to meet his eyes looking at me, "I'm technically a sophomore too, thinking about transferring here. I'm from up north a bit, living with my mom and dad. You like the program?" He talks with such confidence, like the speaker of the house would garner the respect and attention of all of their constituents.

I was beginning to, at this point in my life, acknowledge the simplicity of all things. However, he seemed to know how to easily inch his way under my skin. This and the fact that I didn't have a name to put to the feelings I was beginning to feel in my life. He gave that to me. He continued, taking clear note that I was making silent observations of him.

"Have you ever read anything by Hemingway? Or do you just like his quotes?" he said. I looked again around the room, noticing subtle things I had seemingly never noticed before. A porcelain cow, for example, sat atop one of the shelving units that held coffee bags. The tiles on the floor are black in some places due to a lack of care, and dirt and dust have built up after all these years.

"I do like the program. And, I'll be completely honest with you, I have only heard of the great writer that Hemingway is."

I'm not a talker. I never have been, and I never will be. But I knew the importance of small talk was just that, small. Not only did I not think to ask him a question, but I also didn't really know how. This is what a mindset can do to you; alter the way you exist in your story and in others' stories for the rest of your life. I could've asked, at that moment, "What's your favorite Hemingway story?" I could've asked, "Do you want to read something to me now?" but I didn't. How would he interpret that? My lack of conversational skills? Would he even really care?

"Well, I'd love to get together sometime. To study, or to read together, whatever you'd like. Do you mind if I get your number?" he said, saving me.

I'd been through this before, now, with Abe, with Kell. I hesitated in accepting new friendships from anyone. But, I figured, what the hell. I'm overthinking it too much, it's just a phone number, it's just someone else to talk about literature with.

"Yeah of course. When do you think you'll make the decision to transfer?" I said, pulling out my phone. I press a few times on the screen to get to the add a contact page and pass it over to him.

"I actually just decided." he said, with a coy smile. He doesn't show teeth, but his lips angle themselves to just show a dimple on one side. It is curved, almost, and his lips flatten against his face but they are still full and pink. I notice a small dot on his upper lip, maybe a piece of coffee ground.

I smile back, settling into the comforting idea that this might actually be good.

CHAPTER FOUR
First Date

The next time I saw him, I was better prepared. Months passed, and he had worked through the registration process to get enrolled at our school. He was moving in just blocks from my apartment on 3rd Street. We had been talking the entire time, texting and calling in the evenings. We discussed everything from our favorite books to our deepest fears and hopes.

His was East of Eden. It was a book I hadn't read and had never really cared to read, but after he told me about it, I knew I had to add it to my reading list. He had become my virtual Abe, but better because I didn't have to deal with any of the added weight and burden. We talked on the phone, and that was where I could leave it and continue on with my own life, my own reality. It was nice.

There was one time we had just ended a call and he texted me almost immediately. We never played the "no, you hang up first" game, which I appreciated. His text read "I'm grateful for you" and I could feel all of the butterflies in my stomach start flying up into my throat. So simple and yet so perfect.

I responded, *not as much as I am for you*, with a heart.

He called again, and I answered with a soft hello.

"Only a few more weeks and then I get you see you again," he said. He was whispering.

"I can't wait," I said, smiling through the phone and hoping he could feel it.

"What are you going to do when you see me?" I said, the smile gone from my face and replaced by concern. *Should I have said that?*

"I guess we'll just have to wait and find out," his voice suggested a playful tone, and so the smile returned to my face, "well, I won't keep you. I just wanted to hear your voice one more time. It's time for me to hang up my socks for the night."

It was silent for a few seconds, and then we both exploded into laughter.

"What's the saying for that again?" he laughed again.

"Definitely not hanging up socks," I said, and our laughter carried us into the evening. We didn't hang up that night, at least not either of us intentionally. We talked until we fell asleep, both of our phones lit on the other side of either of our beds, a sad reminder that we were not yet together.

He drove into town on a Friday evening to stay with me before his dad came down at the end of the weekend to help him unpack and set up his new apartment. We had discovered we would be living so close to each other when I sent him my address so he knew where to drive, and we were shocked and delighted at the coincidence it felt to be. As he pulled into the driveway, his bright blue sedan wet and shiny from the rain across the mountains he had just passed to get here, I heard his car sputtered to a stop. I watched from the small window in the front door as he opened his driver's side door, the creak reaching into the house beyond the distance and the walls and into my ears.

I opened the door to greet him, and as I walked toward him, his face was a volcanic eruption of a smile, brilliant white teeth glowing in the overcast day.

"How was the drive," I said and reached out to hug him. *See, I told you I was prepared.* He felt small in my arms, but I knew his arms and back were toned, his muscles contracting against my firm clutch. I tightened my grip around him to feel him for just a bit longer, the smell of his skin radiating off of him, a mix of cologne and sweat from the long drive. He pulled away, and I felt myself get hot from embarrassment.

"Not too bad," he grabbed his backpack from the backseat and looked at me, waiting for me to do something.

"I'm glad to hear that. Let's go inside," I said, "do you need any help bringing anything in?"

He shook his head no and followed behind me into the house.

The afternoon passed quickly, I had driven him around the town and introduced him to the professors that I knew would still be on campus. I told him that I had invited a few friends over for the evening if he was okay with that, to which he agreed immediately. He was a social creature by nature. And so the time came, the drinks and snacks laid out on the kitchen table, and the first knock at the door.

"I'm excited to meet your friends," he said, standing from his seat on the couch. I walked swiftly to the door, opening it to see my friend Kira.

She hugged me tightly, holding two paper bags in her hands. Her energy was wild and optimistic; she was ready to bring the party and bring the best of what this college town had to offer. It was our responsibility, anyway, to put on a good show for the newcomer. She was wearing her high-waisted jeans and flannel with white Converse, a typical outfit for her. Her long reddish-brown hair was halfway down her back, some of it taken up on both sides to make a small ponytail in the back.

She smelled of that familiar smell, old books, and left a whiff of it as she passed by me and introduced herself to Him.

They hugged, and I stood there awkwardly and waited, hoping someone would take over the role of host, but knowing that was not their job. Still, I was excited to bring the two of them together.

"Should we make drinks?" I said, moving towards the kitchen

"Shots?" Kira screamed, her voice raspy and low even through the volume

"I don't usually do shots, but this is a special occasion, right?"

I poured shots of whiskey, Kira's favorite, and we sat on the floor of the living room with our shot glasses. He sat beside me to my right, and Kira sat to my left. His sock-covered toes gently pressed up against my own. I don't think he noticed.

We sat like this for another half hour or so, laughing, drinking, and lightly pressing ourselves against each other, inching closer and closer each minute.

Then, another knock. I knew it was our other friend, Kira's partner Cil. Kira jumped up and raced to the door, leaving Him and I seated and dazed from the swift movement, the alcohol already buzzing in our heads.

The introductions repeated and we all sat back on the floor, the circle bigger now, with Cil now beside me and Kira across from me. The crunch time began for how we would allow our night to play out, whether we would try to find a place to go out to party or just stay in.

"I'd prefer to stay in, if that's alright with you" He said, looking directly at me as if I made the final call.

"I'm okay with that," I had responded, and the others followed suit.

The night fell into a blur of drinking games, laughing, drinking, and curious yet confusing sideways glances at each other to make sure the other was having fun. I felt content watching Him with my friends, seeing how skillfully he was able to converse with them and how graceful his speaking was. He spoke without any stutter, firm and confident yet soft and respectful. He made direct eye contact with anyone whenever they spoke to him and made every intention clear that he was giving them his full attention. It was a mystery to me how, even when he had been drinking, he kept his composure and still remained the greatest at showing others that he cared.

Now dazed and aware of being a bit sloppy, I found myself in the bathroom, alone. I had taken a necessary moment of solitude away from the others, away from the blaring music and chaos of laughter and everyone speaking over the other. I sat on the toilet, pulled my phone out, and snapped a quick picture of my face. For tomorrow, I thought, to look back on. I sat there for a few moments, thinking about nothing in particular.

Just then, a knock at the door of the bathroom. It was Him. He didn't wait for a response before he entered, smiling at me. I was fully clothed, sitting on the toilet. The light was on, brighter than the light in the rest of the house, and I could tell it took him a minute for his eyes to adjust, squinting rapidly at me as his eyes refocused and his pupils dilated.

"Hey just checking on you, everything okay?" he said, with his smile. It was small but confident, that angled smile.

"Yeah, all good. Just needed a break. Do you need the bathroom?" I said, looking up at him. I knew that I probably looked silly. Drunk, a little high, and very exhausted, sitting on the toilet of my bathroom while my friends were playing games in the living room, listening to music, and having a good time. But I didn't feel embarrassed by this, not by him anyhow.

"No, just wanted to check on you," he said, coming into the bathroom and closing the door behind him. I didn't think to stand, the music from outside was now muffled again. I feel a sense of relief. He walks over to me, his hair tousled by the evening, brown waves that cascade a bit over his face leaving strands covering some of his eyes.

"You wanna go for a walk?" he leaned up against the counter, pushing himself up and onto the sink with both of his hands.

I accepted, and we walked out together. The music seemed louder now than it was before, and I felt warm, the alcohol coursing through me. It was a pleasant feeling, one that washed the worry from my mind.

"Where'd they go?" I said as we walked back into the living room. The food and drinks were still on the table, and some of the cups from all of us sitting on the floor had been picked up and moved. We looked around but couldn't find them, so I assumed they had just decided to leave.

"Bring your phone in case they call, but let's go. Show me around your neighborhood" he thought to grab his coat but I decided to go without one, wearing only my shirt and jeans. I slipped on my slides and opened the front door, a gust of cold wind entering the house uninvited.

The night air felt cold but refreshing against my skin. He walked beside me along the road. We stepped into the center, step after step, taking in the quietness of the night and the absence of light besides the few street lamps that were placed without thought around the neighborhood.

In the time that I'd now known him, there wasn't much I had learned. He had a sibling, a younger brother, I believe, that he adored. His parents, divorced, still lived in the same town that they grew up in. They were happy apart but still saw each other almost every day. It's one of those better-as-friends situations. Of course, he loved his parents, he had told me, but he had always felt that they had hidden something from him. Either, maybe, they believed something about him that he didn't yet know about himself or that they didn't see any potential in him at all.

"You know," his tone pulled me out of my thoughts, "when I was younger, I used to take summer trips with my mom to the different haunted hotels around the country." I didn't dare speak, though the thoughts flooded and dipped into the alcoholic haze, then back out, now fuzzy.

I waited, hoping he would fill the silence with something. Eventually, he did.

"It meant a lot to me that my mom would make an effort to understand what I cared about."

I glanced over at him and saw his face; he looked ahead at the road. The grass on the lawns around us was beginning to develop a misty dew on each blade, a phenomenon I knew there was a scientific answer to, but I still liked to imagine was a mystery.

When others shared memories like this with their families, I felt even further away from my own, never in distance, but in soul or in feeling. My parents never understood me, not truly, not wholly. My dad was rarely around, working or training to better support our family and safeguard our future. My mom, a stay-at-home wife, never imagined more for herself than being the caretaker of the home. I think she always lived in her head, never fully accepting what happened to her as a child, and because of that, she never really grew up. It was a relief to hear that others got to experience a mother who was so independent and so self-assured. I wondered if He knew how good he had it, if he was aware of the privilege he had to have parents who both focused on him and his future.

"I wish she knew what it meant to me," he said, turning now to look at me.

"Why don't you tell her?" I responded, now thinking that perhaps my thoughts were misplaced.

"I don't think she would get it. Not really, you know?" he said, his voice trailing off and getting quiet. He turned to me, the air around us now thick.

My body now shivered, not from the cold but from nervous excitement and anticipation. I took a deep breath, the air cold enough to make it visible.

Here he was, standing in front of me, looking effortlessly handsome with a shy smile playing on his lips. His presence alone made my heart race.

"Hey," he said, his voice soft and warm, sending shivers down my spine.

"Hi," I replied, my voice a little higher than I intended. I couldn't help but stare at him, taking in every detail, from the way his hair fell just right to the curve of his lips that I longed to make a move on. I willed him to do something.

"I wanted to tell you this earlier, but I got too nervous," he said, his hands reaching out to hold me. When they touched me, they were surprisingly warm, but I could feel them shiver gently, which sent tingles throughout my body. To be touched by him was a blessing.

"I bought you a bouquet of flowers- carnations- but I left them in the trunk of my car."

"Thank you, but why didn't you give them to me?" I managed to say, my voice barely above a whisper. I could imagine the smell of them as he passed them into my hands, how our fingers would gently touch as they passed from his to mine.

"Well, I didn't know if you felt the same."

With every word he spoke, I found myself falling deeper. I couldn't tell if the alcohol was to blame or if this was actually real, the depth at which I needed him. I marveled at the way his eyes lit up when he talked and the genuine interest he showed in mine.

"Felt the same about what?" I said, knowing that I was egging him on, hoping and praying that this would be the moment I hadn't realized until tonight I had been hoping for all this time. All the conversations, all the calls, even thinking back to that moment in the coffee shop the first time we had met, all led us here. And it meant something.

The neighborhood around us seemed now to be a distant memory; we were far from planet Earth. It was just him and me. His hand found mine, and I felt a jolt of electricity shoot up my arm at his touch. It was a simple gesture, but it spoke volumes, reassuring me that he felt the same way I did.

He spoke again but I stood there, blocking everything out, not being able to help but study his profile, the way his lips moved, the way his eyes sparkled with every expression of his words.

In that moment, time seemed to stand still. The world around us blurred, leaving only him and me. I reached out, my fingers gently tracing the outline of his hand. His eyes were soft with affection.

"Eli, did you hear me?" he said, concern now in his voice. I nodded out of reflex but spoke, "huh?" he laughed.

"I said I felt this strange connection to you ever since that day at the coffee shop, like you and I, together, could achieve something great. Did you ever feel that way?"

I nodded again, this time knowing full well what my intention was.

"I felt like you had. Touching you now, I feel like we fit together like two small grains of rice that had beaten all odds to find one another" he held his gaze at me, now looking at me doe eyed. I didn't quite understand his metaphor, and thought to ask him about it, but before I could, he moved closer. It wasn't the time.

"Eli, can I kiss you?" he said.

My body froze. I knew I wanted to say yes, but what was I supposed to say? What would make this moment more special? Is a yes too simple, too plain? Could it be that if I said yes, he would back away and decide against it?

Instead, I just nodded, seeing now that he was getting uncomfortable from my hesitation.

He moved forward, and our lips met in a tender, sweet kiss, sending a rush of emotions through my entire being.

It was my first moment of intimacy with him, and it felt like the most natural thing in the world. The kiss deepened, and I felt a sense of belonging, a connection that went beyond words. At that moment, I knew I had found something special, something worth treasuring.

We pulled away, both of us breathless, our smiles mirroring the happiness that filled our hearts. We both turned, now hand in hand, and I said, "like two grains of rice."

He laughed and bumped up against me. The air around us had changed, and it buzzed with tension I hadn't experienced before, but I liked it.

I realized that this was just the beginning of something beautiful, something I had never experienced before. With him by my side, I felt like I was dancing on air, and I couldn't wait to see where this newfound love would take us.

CHAPTER FIVE

Immature Love

I knew I loved him when he touched me for the first time. It was a beautiful Saturday afternoon; the butterflies and bees were a flight with their daily duties, and the grass glowed with a vibrant determination for life and for growth. We were beside the creek, watching the water gently lap over the rocks again and over again. Our feet, drying in the droplets of the sun coming in through the trees, were bare and vulnerable. Weeks had passed since our first kiss, and we had decided to take a weekend to drive up to his hometown, a two-hour drive north of our college. I had met his parents for the first time earlier that day.

"It's gorgeous today," he said, grabbing a rock and tossing it into the shallows. It clattered against the pebbles surrounding it and turned black as the water enveloped it.

"It really is," I respond, shyly looking down at my hands, now fumbling with a blade of prairie grass that I had picked along the pathway.

I wanted him to grab me right then. I wanted him to push me to the ground against the rocks and hold me in his arms. That would make today perfect, I thought. His hands fumbled with each other, and I wished that he would make a move towards me. I needed him to make a move, to show me that he felt the way that I felt.

"Hey, look at that," he giggles over a small bird picking a worm from the muddy shore of the creek across from us. To get my attention, he puts his hand on my right foot. I freeze.

This is my moment. I have to return something, anything, so he knows that I don't want this touch to just be one of innocence.

He keeps his hand on my foot and seems to rest it there. Suddenly, I let out a small laugh and inch towards him.

"Probably a mom going to feed her babies," I blurt out stupidly. Still touching my foot, he begins to move his fingers across the bottom and around each toe.

Kiss me. Please.

A few minutes pass until finally he releases my foot from his bizarre massage. What did that mean? My mind began buzzing with thoughts and questions.

He stood. I felt awkward as I stood, thinking about how he hadn't kissed me since that night when we were both drunk in the middle of the street. Maybe he had forgotten; perhaps he had been too drunk to remember.

We walked along the creek a bit longer, both of us barefoot, our feet stumbling across the rocky bed. Every now in then, we would slip, our toes falling into the freezing cold water. His presence, to me, was like a drug. He confused me, exhilarated me, annoyed me, and made me anxious all at the same time and all in the best way possible.

"Eli?" he said finally after a long silence. The only sound before had been the soft trickle of water moving in the opposite direction as us and the pebbles and rocks rearranging beneath our feet.

"Yeah?"

"Do you like me?" he said. I always admired his bluntness and how confident he could be with his words and still speak with such poise and care. My face flushed red with embarrassment. *Why do you even have to ask?* I thought to myself.

"Of course I do; why are you asking me something like that right now?" I responded, sounding harsher than I meant it. My anxiety hit me like a wave; I could feel myself begin to tremble, my mind rushing with the thoughts and scenarios of how I could have done wrong.

"I can't really place it, but I feel like you don't really like me that much. Do you want this?" he replied, quieter this time. I wondered where this was coming from. Had I not shown him how much I cared for him and wanted him in my life? How could I have done a better job at it? And then, my thoughts became more sinister; why hadn't he kissed me? Was it because he was waiting for me to kiss him or was he trying to find a way to talk himself out of any relationship with me by making it seem like it was me that wasn't interested in him?

"Can I kiss you again?" he said, now turning to face me. I was confused by this and took a step back, nodding at the same time.

I could see the pained look on his face as a sign of his embarrassment at my presumed rejection.

"Yes..." I said softly. His face twitched, whether with excitement or frustration, I couldn't quite tell. I could feel my own body hum with apprehension. This was the answer to my question, wasn't it? He wanted me, and I knew I wanted him.

He stepped forward, closing the gap between us, and put his hands on each of my cheeks. They were cold, and I felt as though the heat from my cheeks had transferred from my skin to his fingers.

"Just, be honest with me, okay?" he paused, his brows furrowed and I knew he was contemplating whether or not to say what he was thinking next, "and don't keep all your thoughts to yourself all the time" he leaned closer and pressed his forehead against my own.

Then, he lowered his hands to my shoulders and squeezed, working his way down to my arms and my elbows. He held them there and tilted his head at an angle so that he could kiss me. Our lips pressed against each other, and my body shivered with that familiar tingle. His words rang in my head, entering into every crevice and facet of my mind and lodging there. I had, with everything before, not taken them lightly. I memorialized them and, with them, felt this new aura envelop me. I wanted him more than I had ever wanted him or anyone before. It was, as of this moment, about protection. I wanted to protect this, to protect him from everything else in the world. If he agreed with someone, I wanted to agree with it. If he felt sad about something, I would feel that sadness for him and do everything in my power to make it better.

We stood there for a few minutes, our lips interlocking with each other time and time again.

CHAPTER SIX

Arrival

Pulling into the gravel driveway, thick on either side with trees both bare and fully flush with leaves, we jolted back and forth in our seats. In the distance, about another hundred yards, sat our small summer cottage on the cape. It was beachside, delicately placed in acres of forest. Our neighbors were at least a half mile away on either side, but no direct view to either unless you were sitting on the beach.

Diana, still sitting in the back, perked up as we entered the driveway. She steadied herself on each of our headrests from the gravelly bumps, her head now perfectly centered between us.

A single cool light in the distance, besides the headlights on the car, led the way toward the small breezeway fit for one car. I pulled the car into its position and centered out, quickly changing it into park and turning the car off.

"Marie must have already come by and cleaned for us," Diana says in our ears. Hudson repositions himself, so he is looking at both of us.

"Marie?" he said quizzically.

"Marie lives in the house when we aren't here. When we visit, she takes the guest house, about a quarter mile that way," Diana points ahead and to her right, her arm extending in front of Hudson.

"This is beautiful. Are you sure it isn't a hassle to have me join you? I promise I'll be out of your hair in no time."

Diana smacks him playfully against the chest. He reaches up and rubs the area that she had just touched.

"Don't even think about it," Diana says, "come on, let's get settled."

The single light in the breezeway was our only form of vision as we walked up to the front door. Feeling the crunch of the gravel beneath our feet and the fresh salty air revived me momentarily. We carried our bags up the three wooden steps that creaked as we pressed against them, reaching the door with ease.

The night faded into darkness after that. We quickly showed Hudson to his room for the remainder of his stay and promptly went to our own. What followed was a deep sleep, with its ambiguous dreams of the beach. First, I was alone, sitting on the cobblestone beach in the middle of the day. I could hear someone calling to me, a man's voice, but I didn't dare move my head to either side. Instead, I maintained my gaze directly on the water, on the lapping waves pushing ever closer.

Then, Hudson and Diana were beside me. "It'll be okay, Eli," Hudson spoke gently, leaning in and whispering in my ear. I felt his hand against my back, moving up and down in a fluid and familiar motion.

Then, a gunshot. My vision went red. I assessed my chest first, then felt my arms and down to my legs. Nothing, and yet now the world was awash in red. The sea, now bloody like a strawberry that had burst open and stained the landscape. The sand, darkened into a burgundy, the top layer that was still dry glided across and displaced itself in the wind.

Even with the shot, I felt at ease. I knew someone had taken the bullet, but I didn't hear a scream. I felt it, though. I felt their pain, and I pushed it away into the dark, swirling waters of the sea. The world stood still.

It didn't feel like much time had passed when I was awakened by the sound of the bird-calling clock out in the entryway. The curtain had been pulled back, or maybe it was never closed at all, and the light from the morning sun shone in unfiltered. I squinted my eyes to adjust, pulling the quilt that was on my bed up to my face for warmth. The house was old; it had no central heating. We relied on the chimney in the living room for our supply of heat, but neither Diana nor I had considered that the night before, so it was cold. I swung my legs from the bed and stood on the wood-paneled floor. Thick slabs of old, weathered wood, sanded and smooth with age, my feet welcomed their touch.

The room was unchanged, and yet it felt different. The same bed in the center, the same French doors leading out to the stairs down to the beach. The floor length mirror that was nautical themed stood right beside the door to the hallway that led to the kitchen. From it, I could smell the scent of bacon cooking, and I followed it.

Hudson and Diana were already awake. Diana sat at one of the barstools, her elbows leaning against the island in the center of the kitchen. Hudson sat at the far end of the petrified wood dining table adjacent to the kitchen. They were talking, laughing even, as I entered.

"Good morning, Eli!" Marie said, turning back to the stove, where she continued to prepare breakfast.

"Marie, good to see you," I said, taking a seat beside Diana.

"Eli, good morning! We were just talking about our plans today. Marie was gracious enough to cook us some breakfast, but Hudson elected to go back into town and get us some groceries." Diana looked at me, a cup of coffee in her hand. I could tell she was expecting me to say something, so I didn't.

"I'll go, then, to accompany him. You'll have a few hours to yourself." I looked at Hudson, who still sat at the dining room table, holding his coffee in one hand and a book in the other. He was pretending to read, but I know only moments ago, he was laughing and engaging in conversation with my sister.

He looks up from his book and makes eye contact with me. "Marie told us your neighbors rented out their houses, I guess both are occupied right now." he said, lifting the hand with his book up towards the direction of Marie, now flipping the bacon on the stove.

"Any news from your brother?" I say plainly. I had just woken up; I see no reason to coat my words in kindness or care.

"I sent him a few messages this morning, but nothing. I'm sure he's just gotten a hotel somewhere in town and will respond to me by the time we get back."

After a while, we ate. I made myself a cup of coffee. Marie had prepared for us a feast of scrambled eggs, orange juice, fruit with feta, bacon, and English muffins. I took a helping of everything, making sure to give my extra thanks to the chef.

A few hours alone sounded perfect and a necessary respite after the long drive with both my sister and a stranger. Diana and Hudson offered to take an Uber so as to leave me the car in case I needed it for whatever reason, but I insisted they take the car. I would stay here, I told them, and get some work done. Plus, if I did need to go anywhere, Marie would be friendly enough to offer me her car.

When they left, I felt the profundity of their absence. The house felt lifeless, void of sound and warmth. Moments after their departure, I put some wood in the furnace and sat beside it for a while. On the wall behind me was a collection of prints in miscellaneous frames. The living room was built like an a-frame, with a long wooden beam going across the top at an angle. That meant that the ceiling on one side was much higher than the other, and the frames reached every open spot around the entire wall. To my left was the dining room and kitchen, which also led to the greenhouse and deck down to the beach. To my right was the hallway I had emerged from this morning, as well as the front door.

As the air around me began to warm, as did my skin against the heat of the metal furnace, I felt a sense of calm wash over me. No responsibilities or expectations here. The carpet, faded and brown with its age and lack of care, was precisely where it belonged. In the city, an environment like this would never be accepted. Clean, modern spaces were the expectation. But here, it was the old, the forgotten, the dirty that brought a sense of warmth and comfort. There was no comfort in the city, and yet living here could not be a reality for an innovative person or for an intellectual. *Maybe when I retire*, I think to myself, almost laughing at my own thoughts.

I didn't intend to do work while they were gone. Instead, I had brought a book with me to my space beside the furnace. The cover was missing, the pages brown and tattered, and yet it was still the only copy I would ever read. It had been a gift from so long ago.

I opened to the page I was at and fell directly into the world. It was a familiar feeling but one that I had never and would never get used to. Like a black hole that delivers you into a world adjacent to our own, to a place that exists but doesn't. To a character who could be living the exact same life as you somewhere else in the world at this very moment. But it isn't. What a beautiful thing that is.

Leon lived in Raleigh, North Carolina. He was born only miles from the city, had gone to college in the city, and now lived as a professional in the city. His wife, Marley, and their three kids lived with him. They had a humble life, with a five-bedroom home in a suburb of the city. They took daily walks with their golden retriever, Gus, and enjoyed dinner at 5:30 p.m. each night as a family. Leon was happy; he hadn't known anything else. On a typical Tuesday afternoon, after saying goodbye to the kids and his beautiful wife, still asleep in bed, Leon got in his ten-odd-year-old Toyota Camry and drove. He passed through the houses in his small neighborhood and could already hear the hustle and bustle of the traffic in the heart of the city. Not even six in the morning, and the world was already awake, calling to him. Today, though, he would not answer the call. He took the usual route to work, feeling the obligation to at least pass his firm on the way toward his destination. He thought to himself, as he passed the building lit with his name, if it was worth it. All the hard work, all the effort put into building his own firm and raising a family of his own. All of it would stay in Raleigh. It, just like him, would be born, would live, and would die in Raleigh. Nothing would come of it, and in a hundred years, his name would be all but forgotten. Sure, his children would live on in his name for a time until even his grandchildren or their children stopped talking about him.

He could feel the weight lift from him as he drove out of the city and into the hills, out into the place where he could feel free. A fleeting feeling, yes, but one he wanted to feel on his last day on earth.

I looked up from my book at the sound of the door creaking open, Diana and Hudson walking in with bags up to their elbows of food and supplies. I felt a tinge of whiplash from the interruption, having been ripped from Leon's world and brought back into my own. I followed them both with my eyes as they hobbled over towards the kitchen, hoisting the bags about their waist and dropping them down with a thud on the island counter.

"Did you buy out the whole store? I joke, still seated.

They laughed, and I stood, walking over to them to help them with the groceries. We talked about our plans for the rest of the day and our intentions for the trip. Diana and I discussed staying for at least another week, and when she proposed the idea, I was reminded to call Greg back about his invitation to work together on a thesis topic. I knew it was what Diana wanted, to stay another week, but it would have been so much easier if she had just told me about her plans before leaving so that I wouldn't feel so trapped in this space with her.

The groceries had been put away and we had settled into our plans. Hudson had decided that he needed to connect with his brother, who had flown into town around the same time as us. He was going to drive and meet him, so Diana decided that would be a good opportunity for us to take a sibling walk to the beach.

It took a few minutes to change but once I had, Diana was waiting for my on the back porch. She had changed as well, now wearing a puffer vest with a pair of black leggings. She had her hair up in a bun on the top of her head. When I opened the door, she smiled at me and put her phone back in her pocket.

We walked for a few minutes in silence as we descended onto the beach. It was midday, overcast, and the waves were coming in fast, crashing against the hard, wet sand. There was a chill in the air, so I clutched my jacket a bit tighter around my body. *Oh, how much things have changed,* I thought. We walked on the wet part of the sand, dodging the waves as they came in. I was surprised at Diana's silence but knew it wasn't my place to start a conversation. So, I went deeper into my own mind. It was enough for me just to be able to walk on the beach with her; there was no added benefit to talking. There couldn't be.

Suddenly, she stopped and turned to the waves.

"Let's go in," she said, already removing her shoes and socks. I shook my head no and watched as she took steps forward, allowing a wave to rush up against her shins, splashing against them. I could see her entire body tense up, and she laughed.

I took my socks and shoes off as well and joined her.

"Do you remember that one summer you got your leg caught in an abandoned house?" she said, kicking up some of the loose sand that her weight had created against the current.

"Yeah, how could I forget? I still have the scar to prove it happened, and it was one of my more embarrassing memories," I said, my feet falling further and further into the stand.

She sighed deeply, her breath a white mist as it exited her body.

"You always overthought everything. Do you still do that?" she said, her voice faltering against the sound of the waves.

"I try not to. Why?"

"You just don't even talk much anymore; sometimes, I think you're too far trapped in your own head. You used to wear your feelings on your sleeve."

I nodded slowly, hoping to make clear to her that to me, that was a good thing that I had learned to keep my feelings away and hidden from everyone. And, more than that, why did she care?

"I just want to know that you are happy, is all…" I thought she was going to say more, but her voice was lost to the waves for a moment.

We stood in silence as the waves washed over our feet, sand entangling itself in the lower hem of our pants. I looked out to the ocean and noticed a place, not too far off, where the water seemed calmer. That is where I wanted to be, in that quiet place among all the waves around it.

"That day," she began, "when you got your leg caught. That day was the day that I knew you were the strongest person I would ever meet. I don't know when, but I think at some point, you became so strong you forgot to feel. Isn't that a tragedy? To escape all of your emotions and just simply to exist?"

I didn't respond.

"I'm leaving William," she blurted out, "and I could use some of your strength right now."

She turned and walked back in the direction of the house, leaving her shoes and socks on the beach in the sand. I knew she wanted me to follow her, but I was content where I was. And now, I had something to reflect on, to press into my soul and memorialize it, hardening it to stone.

CHAPTER SEVEN
First Time

It became a routine for us to drive up to his hometown. It was a place of safety for both of us. For him, it was where most of his memories were, and he reveled in being able to share them with me. For me, it was a place that I knew meant something to him. And so, it meant something to me. After our last class, we would pack a duffle bag and drive up on Fridays. His mom's house, where we would usually stay, was about an hour and a half away from our homes at college. He always drove, and I would watch him, staring intently at the road ahead, his brows furrowed. It was the only time I actually saw him worry, or at least look worried, and I had decided it was because he cared so much for me; he knew it was an important responsibility to have me with him in the car.

This time was exceptional. It was Friday, and we had a long weekend. I was also our six months, though neither dared jinx it by speaking it out loud. During the drive, I thought maybe he hinted at it by playing our favorite song, the first song that played when we met, *Palm Trees*. It was not a song that fit us or our relationship, but it was our first song, and that counted for something. Every aspect of our relationship mattered, it felt. Every moment we shared, every gift or glance or words exchanged.

He reached out his hand and placed it on the inside of my left thigh. I tensed up, and I knew he noticed because he eased his grip. Instead, he lightly pressed his fingers against the fabric of my jeans. I trembled at the feeling. I decided to lean into it, and I lifted my leg against his hand, hoping that would prompt him to hold tighter. It wasn't that I didn't want him to hold my leg, but, I don't know, maybe I wasn't used to it? It happened every time he did it, though.

After some time, we arrived at his mom's house. It was a long house, maybe two hundred feet in length, with a built-in swimming pool that had been built for him and his brother growing up. His parents treated him like an only child; it was as if he didn't even have a brother. We walked in with our bags and were greeted by his mother. An older woman with long, graying blond hair that still cascaded across her shoulders. She looked weathered, like the house that was built by her now ex-husband and His father. Her hair was a mess about her face; it was like she hadn't brushed or washed it in weeks. Her hands were calloused, and her nails were caked with dirt. She wore a cream-colored blouse with khaki pants, a look that did not match her appearance.

When she spoke, it was clear she had been a long-time smoker. Her voice was raspy and harsh but somehow comforting, too.

"Eli! It is so good to see you again," she said, opening her arms wide to envelop me in a hug. Her breasts were large, and they pressed up tightly against my thin frame. They added to the feeling of comfort that she emanated, she was warm and smelled of smoke and cedar. It was a soft smell, covered over by her sweet vanilla and spice perfume.

"Okay, you two, I've gone to the grocery store for you both, the fridge is fully stocked. I'll be upstate about an hour away, Dan got us a beautiful little cottage, so if you need anything just give me a call." she smiled at me before looking over at Him and winking.

"Dan?" I said, smirking at her.

"Oh, my goodness, Eli, come sit! I have to show you some pictures, and then I will get out of your hair, I promise!" she glances again at Him before ushering me over to her small standing kitchen table in the middle of the room between the living room and kitchen.

She pulled out her phone and started scrolling through her camera roll, showing me pictures of the cabin that she was going to for the weekend and then pictures of her and Dan, who I learned is her new boyfriend. I thought to ask Him about that later, once she left.

"Is he coming to get you?" he said inquisitively. She nodded and started to walk away.

"I'll leave you both to get settled. He should be here soon, so if I don't see you when I leave, have a great weekend!" I thought what she had said was odd considering it was a one-story house and there would be no reason for us not to say goodbye to her when she left, but I decided against it, realizing it didn't really matter.

Once she had left, I looked at him. He rolled his eyes at me and offered a weak smile.

"I didn't know she was giving us the house the weekend? That was kind of her."

"She wouldn't if it weren't for Daniel," he said under his breath. I wasn't sure where his tone was coming from. He had a habit of saying everyone's full name, except for mine, when he mentioned them. I think to him, it was a matter of respect, but in this case, it seemed like he was scolding his mom's new boyfriend. He grabbed my hand and pulled me towards his bedroom, at which point he closed the door behind him.

His room hadn't changed since he was a child, and it was a pleasure for me to see the memorabilia he still had and the stories he would talk about regarding the various items around the room. On one wall was a full-size upright piano. Above that were two extended shelves covered in action figures, loose books, and posters from various places around the state that he had visited. Once, I noticed a poster from the Stanley Hotel in Colorado, and he told me about its history of hauntings. It was that year, he said, that his mom took him there and told him that she was divorcing his father. He had always thought it was because she was cheating but could never prove it, and he wished she hadn't told him then because it became clear that was the only reason for the trip.

On the adjacent wall was his desk, covered in scraps of paper, calligraphy pens, and random ramblings of his writing. I knew he was a writer, but he had never shared any of his writing with me. He romanticized his writing by telling me all about his muses and the authors from whom he absorbed inspiration, so much so that when I read their work, I would imagine it was his own.

Across from the piano was his bed, against a long window that looked out to the driveway. On the end of the bed was a quilt that his aunt had made him. She was a woman I knew he respected deeply but didn't talk often about. I never knew what became of her, but conversations brought up about her were usually diverted.

His bed. A large mattress pushed up against the corner of the room, with no bedframe or headboard; the sheets and blankets always smelled slightly of him, slightly of dust from lack of a body sleeping in it. I would imagine, as I slept in his childhood bed, the times he would sleep here after school, after a soccer game, or after a school play. How many times had he slept in just his boxers or without his boxers? How many of his friends had sat on this bed or slept on this bed with him? How many people had he brought into this bed for something more?

The sheets were red, something we now laughed at whenever we saw them. He had once told me, when I asked him why they were red, that red was the color of sex and the bed was the sexiest part of any bedroom so the sheets had to reflect that. I remember feeling a tinge of jealousy at hearing that but soon I calmed down and realized the comedy in it. How could I be jealous of a bed?

"You need to get a bedframe," I said, plopping my duffle bag down by the door and sitting on the edge of the bed, feeling the quilt with my fingers.

"I have one. It's in the other room. One time, my friend was over, and he tackled me onto the bed, and it completely split the bedframe in half with the weight of both of us," he responded. I didn't say anything. Instead, I let gravity take me, and I fell backward against the cushioned mattress.

On the ceiling were little plastic glow-in-the-dark stars. He had a fascination with stars, I don't know why. Literature and stars.

He joined me on the bed and we slept for a while.

When I woke up, it was dark. I was alone in the room, but I smelled something warm coming from the kitchen. Spices filled my nose as I opened his bedroom door all the way. He must have left it cracked open when he escaped, perhaps knowing that the smell would wake me up.

I walked out into the kitchen, rubbing the sleep from my eyes. He had, in the center of the living room, created a fort for us. I mentioned months ago how adults never seemed to do the things that kids loved doing so deeply. It brought joy, I had said, for adults to give in to their childish fantasies every now and again.

"What's all this?" I said, scaring him out of his position in the kitchen over the stove.

"Oh good, you're awake! I need your help," he said, walking toward me.

He walked past me, giving me a brief peck on the way, squeezing my shoulders gently, and into his bedroom.

"Help me move this into the fort," he said, grabbing his mattress.

I didn't ask questions. He knew what he was doing. I joined him, and we awkwardly grabbed hold of the mattress and half-pulled and half-carried it into the living room under the blankets he had delicately placed. They were one push away from falling in on us, so we made sure to be careful. Once we had it placed where he wanted it, he said, "Dinner should be ready soon. I think you're really gonna like it. Then, I have a surprise for you."

I looked at him, "isn't the fort surprise enough?" I giggled, following him back out the way we came, now crawling slowly. I grabbed his foot on the way out and scratched it, making him laugh back at me.

I settled at the kitchen table. He had placed plates, utensils, and napkins next to each other. In the middle sat a tall white candle and a small vase with two green carnations. The candle was unlit and yet the room had a warm yellow glow about it. I sat down at one of the four barstools that sat out around the kitchen table. He came over behind me and wrapped his arms around my stomach, squeezing tightly.

"What do you think?" he said. I knew he was proud of himself, but part of me felt discomfort at his physical touch. For a moment, I wondered if he just wanted me to stroke his ego or if he genuinely wanted to know what I felt about it.

"It's perfect. Thank you for putting this together," I said, turning my head slightly to see his face.

He kissed my forehead and moved his face, leaning his forehead against mine.

"I wanted to do this. For you," he says, and his lips touch mine. This kiss felt different than all the others, both from him and from those before him. It was more mature, deeper than one I had ever felt before.

We hung there, suspended in the air of our love, with our lips still locked together. Neither of our mouths opened and yet we gave to each other exactly what the other needed to feel the love pour between the two of us.

Finally, I pulled away gently, and he smiled at me, his cheeks now flushed red.

Sometime later, we sat down for dinner. It was some sort of roast with greens and mashed potatoes. We smiled at each other the entire time, not daring to glance down at our food for more than a second so as not to miss any moment together. Periodically, he would reach his hand across the table at me, closing the void between us that felt endless, and hold my hand.

"Thank you again for this," I said to him as we placed the dishes in the dishwater. I awkwardly squeezed his left bicep as his hands worked the sink, spraying the dishes down with soap and water.

"It's not over yet," he said, a smile spreading wide across his face. I felt full, both in my heart and in my stomach, without a worry in the world at this moment. I couldn't imagine what he meant, but I waited, sitting back at the kitchen table, and took momentary stock of my life.

I thought about Kell and Abe in this moment, while sitting at the kitchen table of my boyfriend's mom's house, thinking about what they must be doing in this exact moment while I was living out the dream I always thought I had wanted with each of them. Every memory, every moment, had brought me to this moment here, with Him. And it was worth it. The heartbreak, the regression back to isolation each time rejection struck, ending without closure.

It was Him. It was all for Him.

I am not sure how much time passed before he came over behind me again, this time massaging my shoulders. He leaned down over to my ear and said "Can you come join me in the fort, please?" and grabbed my hand swiftly. We crawled together into the fort and onto the mattress, on which we had put multiple blankets and pillows from around the house. We lay down next to each other and turned inward into each other.

"Do you ever think about the first day we met?" he said, touching my barefaced cheek, and rubbing his thumb gently across the natural line of my cheekbone.

"All the time," I whispered, "what specifically, though?"

He shook for a moment with a silent laugh; the only sound that came from him was a short huff of air.

"Just how coincidental it was. A moment so simple that changed our lives in multiple different ways."

I nodded, processing what he had said.

"I want you to know, Eli, how important you are to me." his smile faded. I knew he wanted to be serious.

"You don't give yourself enough credit to the person that you are. You are brilliant" he said, tracing the outline of the tattoo on my chest now, pushing the collar of my shirt further down to reach every part of it. My skin responded to his touch. There was sadness in his voice, but it was far from negative.

"Getting to know you has been the single most apotheosis of my life." he smiled again, aware of the absurdity of using such a complex word in conversation.

I reached my arm under his and around his back, up his shirt. I gently itched his back with my nails, feeling each part of his skin.

"You know I'm not great with my words," I began, "but you make my words feel important. And when I say I love you, I mean I really love you. I have never understood the gravity of that word until I met you."

He scooted closer to me, every inch of our body touching.

"Can I kiss you, Eli?" he said, and we both laughed.

He leaned in for a kiss, and I could feel my body tense and become hot. My denim jeans were becoming uncomfortable as we lay here so close to each other. It felt wrong to be clothed next to him.

He pulled away and looked into my eyes. They were glistening in the little light that we had in the fort, and I could see myself in them. Beyond his milky brown irises, I saw the vast galaxy of stars. He was a galaxy, a universe, and I was finally seeing him. The answers were finally within reach.

"Are you ready for your last surprise?"

I nodded.

He lifted himself up off the mattress, careful not to hit his head on the blanket above us. He crawled out of the fort and a few moments later, re-entered with a small tv and two pairs of pajamas.

I couldn't help but laugh. He handed me my pair and set up the TV at the end of the mattress. The pajamas were a pair of blue shorts with white drawstrings, the hem reaching just above my knees. I pulled my legs from my jeans and changed quickly into the new shorts, which were soft and cozy cotton.

Once we had settled back down, he turned the TV on and configured it to play a movie.

When the title screen appeared, I looked at him with a playful annoyance, cocking my head and rolling my eyes.

"How could you have remembered that I liked this movie?" I said, nudging him with my foot. He was still at the edge of the mattress, after just having clicked play he crawled back toward me and placed a kiss on my lips.

"I'm very observant, you know. Plus, I thought it would be a perfect time for me to watch it for the first time. With you."

I smiled and turned, wrapping my leg over his and laying half on top of him. I kissed him hard on the lips, allowing my body to melt into his, each muscle relaxing one after the other.

The movie, now on in the background, played the familiar tune that was recognizable even for those who have never seen it, even those who had never heard of it.

I wanted to watch, but attending to him was more important. I was overwhelmed by this feeling of warmth around us. The blankets that surrounded us reflected the flashing lights from the screen and, erupting our space in a flurry of color; red, orange, black, yellow, and brown flashed around us, changing every second.

"Are you happy?" he said, pushing me off of him gently and replacing my position with his own. His face loomed over me now, and I couldn't help but smile. The skin around my lips pulled tight. He was on top of me, straddling my pelvis, and I felt my body heat up even more.

I nodded, leaning my head up to meet his lips. My arms wrapped around his back and down the curvature of his spine until I was at the small of his back. I reached underneath his shirt and pulled it upward, feeling the soft cotton float off his skin and above his head. I tossed it beside me, and he returned the favor.

Now both shirtless, he surveyed my upper half, both with his eyes and his fingers. He kissed my lips and moved with his tongue slowly up and around to my ear, breathing slow but deep.

"I love you," he whispers in my ear, and my entire body shivers with anticipation.

I try to sit up, to turn him over and take control, but he pushes me back down.

"It's my turn, tonight. Let me take care of you." he spoke breathlessly, as if these were the last words he would ever utter, or even want to utter.

He resumed his flurry of kisses, now moving down the curve of my neck. It was sloppy, his kisses, but well placed, each sending a lightning strike straight down to the area within my shorts, growing ever hotter.

His tongue moved down across my nipples, one after the other, and followed slowly down the center of my stomach until he reached the top of my shorts. He jumped off briefly, only giving me enough time to pull my shorts down and off. I attempted to help him by pulling my legs from each of the leg holes, but it only resulted in making the action more awkward. He laughed and tossed them aside to lie by our crumpled shirts.

Now, back on me, he pulled his shorts down as well, with ease. He leaned down and kissed me, the warmth spreading throughout my body, reaching his, and coming back again.

"Tonight, I want all of you. And I don't ever want to let it go." He reached his hand back, and after a moment, euphoria erupted within me. His breath became shallower, and I could tell that mine did as well, but I wasn't so clear as to why.

His kisses became more passionate and deep, and with each kiss, he pushed his tongue deeper into my mouth, lifting himself off my body and back on again.

We kept at this for a few moments, my arms wrapped around his back, holding him, his body moving and trembling with the love we shared.

He felt like home. In this moment, we were more than just the galaxy of stars, we were the answer to the entire universe. We were one complete person, together, linked now completely in body and in mind.

"How do you feel," he asked, still breathless, as he pulled me up closer to him.

I responded with, "I love you," and in that moment, we both burst like a spontaneous combustion of chemicals mixing together, finally reaching their final point of resistance.

The part of me that was mine and now swirled in him stayed there as he slid off of me, now holding me in his arms.

This was the beginning of my downfall.

CHAPTER EIGHT

The Moments Before

Our love sprouted and grew even further from that point on. We became inseparable, so much so that no one knew my name without having mentioned his, and the same the other way around.

The school year had all but come to an end, and I knew I would be finishing Sophomore year on the honor roll again. It was something worth celebrating, I knew, but I had never been great at sharing my accomplishments with others. After my last final of the week, I walked out of the language building on campus and into the bright and sunny day. The building was brick, five tall stories, shaped like a tenement building from the outside. The elevator had never worked since I'd started taking classes in it, and it was one of the oldest buildings in the university, one that had never received enough funding to remodel.

Even with all of this, it was still my favorite building. At least it had a history; at least it had a story. No one could say the same about any of the newer buildings; they could never feel that homey connection to their primary building.

As if on cue, my phone rang as I walked the path toward the nearest student parking lot.

"Hey babe" His voice came through from the other end of the phone, that soft angelic voice. I smiled and said "Hi baby, I just got out of my final. You ready?"

We were going to away for the weekend, to celebrate completing the year together. It wasn't so much "away" as it was a staycation.

"Yeah, I'm just finishing up my last essay now, and then I'll turn it in. Do you want to meet me at the student union in thirty? I'll bring my stuff, and we can leave from there."

I was surprised he hadn't asked about my final, so I thought I would prompt him by asking about his.

"That sounds good, I'm going to go pick up my stuff and I'll wait for you at the coffee shop. How's the essay coming?" he sighed loudly, and paused.

"Stressful," he said finally, "I'll tell you about it when I see you. I gotta go." I thought he was just going to hang up on me because he paused for a long moment. My throat started to choke up, and I could feel a lump form in the back of my throat.

"I love you," he said, and my anxiety eased. The sun still shone above me.

Every call he made to me ended this way, with a pause and a bye and then an *I love you*. It was the highlight of any call he made to me, but this time I felt a heightened sense of anxiety. *Why?*

When I arrived at the student union, I found a seat upstairs and sat, pulling out my phone. It wasn't much longer before he arrived, and behind him was one of his friends. He was wearing his blue ripped jeans, converse, and button-up shirt. On his head was a backward blue hat. His friend, who trailed quickly behind him, was wearing similar clothing, a pair of black ripped jeans, a flannel, and black Converse. Over the flannel hung a jacket that looked too familiar; I had to double-take for it to click; it was His.

"Hi, Eli!" his friend said as they approached. He walked over to me and gave me a quick hug, and I knew something was wrong. He pulled away.

"You remember Jeremy," he said, pointing over to his friend hesitantly like he was embarrassed.

I knew what was coming, but I didn't know how to be prepared for it.

"He needs a ride home; his parents canceled on him." Jeremy smiled, and I smiled back at him, knowing that this was not his fault. I nodded slowly, knowing what this meant for our trip.

"Okay, what do you want to do?" I said. I felt like he needed to solve this, and it was his job to make everyone happy in this situation if he wanted to take his friend home. We already had this plan, why should I have to sacrifice it?

The fluorescent lights beamed brightly overhead and I could feel a slight headache coming on.

"Well, I'll go drive him home and then come back. Then, we'll pack up and leave, I promise" He was asking for me to deal my cards out on the table, he left me with no other option. With Jeremy here, I couldn't say no to him. It would make me look bad. But, if I said yes, I couldn't very well text him later and tell him that I was upset.

God, why was he putting me in this situation in the first place?

"Okay, I will wait at my place, then? You can just text me when you are on your way back."

He smiled and kissed my cheek, leaving behind a red mark of embarrassment.

"Have a great summer, Eli," Jeremy said sweetly. As they walked away from me, I felt in my heart that he was walking away from me in more ways than one. I pushed the thought out of my head, or at least tried to.

I waited in the student union for another fifteen minutes before leaving myself, driving back to my house, and unpacking my weekend duffle bag.

The day had passed slowly, but the sun had gone from the sky, and the only light coming from outside my bedroom window was the soft glow of the bright white moon. I had unpacked my clothes, and the duffle bag sat limp on my bedroom floor. I was in the house alone, and I sat in my bed in my own warmth. A book sat next to me, one of his copies, and I had reached for it once I got home, having every intention of reading some of it before drifting off into a midafternoon nap.

I checked my phone for a text or call from him, and there was nothing. I wanted to wait for something from him; after all, that is what he said he would do when he was on his way home. I leaned over my bed and flipped the switch to my sunset lamp. Once I did, the room illuminated in a deep ombre of orange and red. I felt comforted by this.

I began to think and to wonder, my thoughts falling deeper and deeper into a dangerous hole of paranoia. Like a cave, my mind has thoughts that went further and wedged themselves in the cracks and crevices of the walls of the cave, leaving less space for others to make their way out alive. Eventually, they clogged the entire system, and there was no room left to think.

I breathed in deeply and exhaled. What if he got in a car accident? What if this was it, and he was cheating on me? Why would he cheat on me? Why was Jeremy wearing his jacket? He must be cheating on me.

Suddenly, the white light on my phone lit up and contrasted against the orange glow. I quickly reached for it and looked at the notification; it was Him.

It read: *Hey, I am so sorry for being late, there was so much traffic. On my way back now. I love you.*

Everything in my body relaxed; my nerves and muscles now slack against my mattress sheets. I liked the message and responded quickly.

Get home safe, please. I love you, too.

I waited a few minutes and thought to send another text,

I'll wait up for you. Do you want to sleep at mine tonight?

I put my phone down and expected him to take a while to respond if he was driving. Instead, the phone lit back up almost immediately.

Yes, babe. I'll be there in an hour.

CHAPTER NINE

The Beach

It was the next day. I hadn't spoken to Diana or Hudson for the remainder of the evening. Hudson had come home late from spending time with his brother, and I am sure he and Diana gushed all about it. I, on the other hand, went to my room to read. Now, as the morning light shone through the windows of my room, I knew I should get up.

When I walked out into the hallway, I noticed the house was eerily quiet. There was a note on the kitchen island that read:

Eli, Hudson, and I went to take a walk and enjoy the beach for a bit. There are muffins still warm in the oven. Grab one and come join us.

-Di

I smiled briefly before realizing how silly it was to do so alone in the kitchen. I took note of two mimosa glasses and an empty orange juice and champagne bottle. They were most likely already drunk, and it hadn't even passed midday. I had slept in.

I changed quickly and grabbed the muffin from the fridge. It was a coffee cake muffin topped with brown sugar. I walked down the path to the beach and noticed a grouping of rock irises in bunches of weeds on the way down. I decided to stop for a moment to pick some. *No need to rush*, I thought to myself.

Once I had a good bundle, I continued my trek down to the beach. It was a crisp and clear day; the ocean was calm and glassy, and the sun above was reflecting off of it. Its reflection left a bright blue glow in the air, probably one that added to the crispness that it felt like.

I saw them halfway down the beach, Hudson was fully entrenched in the water, and Diana sat in the sand with a blanket, their belongings. As I approached, Diana noticed me and smiled.

There wasn't anyone else on the beach besides us and a few neighbors, but they were further on still. I told Diana I wanted to go give them my salutations, and she nodded, the smile vanishing from her face.

As I walked further down toward the cliffs toward the end of the beach, there was a small stream that flowed nicely from a few of the jagged rocks further up towards land. The closer it got to the ocean, the bigger it got, and so I walked up toward the cliffs so I could more easily step over it without getting wet.

When I walked up, there was a look of surprise on their faces. They were newer members of the neighborhood if you could even call it that, and they had traveled all the way from some part of Europe. I had only introduced myself once before, so I figured it polite to do it again.

The husband was playing a small flute for his wife and another man that I can only assume would be a friend. Their two children, both under ten, swam in the shallow part of the water. The wife was keeping a lazy eye on them, more enthralled in the music her husband was serenading her with.

"Hi! My name is Eli. Eli Greene." I said plainly. Even this seemed out of character for me, and I began to wonder why I had done it. And, beyond that, why had I only said my name. It was too late now, I thought, so it was better to just drop it.

"Good afternoon," the wife said, looking up at me. She covered her eyes with her hand from the sun. I could feel it beat against me with more brilliance that before and I began to sweat.

She had a strange accent, one I could not place.

"We have met before. I just thought it best to introduce myself again. Have a great day," I said and began to turn when the man stopped his flute to speak.

"Thanks for saying hi! We don't see many people out here, what with all the short-time stayers and renters," he said, and I turned back to smile.

"My sister, Diana, and I are just here for a week before heading back into the city. It is nice to get away." I made a point to finish my sentence with clear finality. They smiled back at me, and before walking away, I glanced at the third person, the other man, who looked at me pensively.

I chose to ignore it and walked back to where Diana was sitting. Now, Hudson had joined her. He was wearing a pair of swim shorts, and he had taken his shirt off. Instead, a towel was wrapped around his broad shoulders.

"Eli! Welcome back," he said, the enthusiasm in his voice exhausting.

I looked at him and feigned a smile. I was sitting down on Diana's other side, so she sat in the middle between us.

"How was your morning?" I leaned forward and looked at them both. The air was warmer now, but I am sure Hudson felt cold from the seawater. My t-shirt and shorts were sufficient enough, however, to enjoy the weather without any discomfort.

Diana laughed quickly, "We woke up pretty early to make breakfast, then at some point we just started making mimosa's and didn't really stop. And now, here we are." she pulled a bottle of champagne from the back behind her and pushed it toward me, "do you want some?" I accepted.

"At least one good thing came out of this incredibly crazy trip," Hudson said, "I got to drink with two awesome people on a beach in Cape Cod."

I assumed that this meant that maybe the meeting with his brother hadn't gone as well as he had hoped. Then again, perhaps he shouldn't have expected that much from his brother, considering his past track record and Hudson's sentiments about him in the car.

I looked out to the ocean, still beautifully clear, and wondered if he was silent because he was waiting for me to speak. I look over at him and see that he is smiling, and there is a hazy glaze over his eyes. The waves reflect off of them perfectly, leaving a shine I have only ever seen once before.

"Oh, and Eli, Hudson is going to stay with us for the rest of the week. We should have another rental car delivered by then, and then we can head back over into the city." Diana looked at me and smiled. I wasn't sure if she was trying to play a game with me, considering we hadn't talked about the information that she shared the night before. Now, she was trapping me for even longer, saying that we had to wait for the new rental car so that we could leave.

The sun beat down even harder still, and I could feel beads of sweat begin to form on my hairline. It was cause for my annoyance.

Some time passed, and as it did, the sun rose higher in the sky. The morning chill had completely burnt off. The air felt thick with moisture, and my shirt was now damp from sweat.

Between the three of us, we had finished the bottle of champagne and I could feel the liquid warm my insides even more, my head having fogged over. I decided to lay down on the blanket and allow the sun to have full coverage over my body. The waves were lapping a bit harder now, the sound of them almost lulling me into a dreamlike state.

Hudson swam more and Diana pulled out her phone to do God knows what, but I tried to drown them out as well. It wasn't until some more time passed that I felt the air around us change once again. It became a bit colder; the wind had picked up just a bit.

Diana then mentioned that it might be a good idea to go back inside, so we all gathered our belongings and began our trek back up to the cabin.

As we walked, I noticed a few more people on the beach. There was another family some ways in front of us that had set up an umbrella and were having a nice afternoon under the sun. These kids seemed to want to opt out of swimming and instead played with a ball along the wet sand, the sound of it skidding across reaching my ears.

Then, there was a man.

He was alone, walking toward us. I couldn't make out much of his features, but it looked as if he had come out from near where our cabin was. I thought it was peculiar, but of course, who am I to question anything.

"There he is! Both of you, I'd like you to meet my brother." Hudson said, pointing to the man. We continued walking closer and closer to the man. My feet dragged in the sand; the sun, although now beginning to fall from the sky, still gave off a heat that had now become unbearable.

"Thanks again, Diana," Hudson said, and he ran up ahead to meet his brother.

"Thanks again?" I said, and Diana looked at me.

"Yeah, I told Hudson he could invite his brother over for dinner. He offered to cook for us. Eli, it's okay."

I huffed and wiped the sweat from my forehead.

"Great," I mumbled.

"They're leaving at the end of the week, anyway. Hudson had this whole thing planned; he's going to ask his brother today to join him on a backpacking trip around Europe. I guess it has been a dream for both of them. He told me all the details last night while you were in your room."

I was no longer paying attention to her. We were close enough now, with both Hudson and his brother walking toward us, that I recognized him.

He had grown out of his Converse and ripped jeans wearing days and instead wore a pair of white flannel pants, sandals, and a loose-fitting Henley shirt. His hair was longer, still wavy in some areas, but wilder and more tousled than it had been before. Somehow, though, it all made him look older and more mature. And, I guess he was, after more than ten years, that is what you can expect from someone; to change.

The closer we approached, the easier I could see the expression on his face change. He was laughing with Hudson but, once he saw me, the lines around his mouth straightened out and the lines on his forehead appeared, his brows furrowed.

I look at Diana and even her face has changed. She knew. *How has this happened?*

It really was Him.

CHAPTER TEN
Moments After

Weeks passed into the summer, and we both went our separate ways, vowing to see each other as often as possible. Otherwise, we would work, stay with family, and visit with friends who were also home for the summer. It was one of the hottest summers we had yet, with record-level temperatures beating each other daily.

I was sitting on the back deck of our summer home, the sun beating down and covering my skin in a thin layer of sweat, glistening off its light. I had set up my station with my book, laptop, a glass of water, and a glass of white wine. I felt inspired today, so I thought I would take advantage of that and the weather by working on an idea for a grouping of short stories that had been born in one of my creative writing courses.

He was joining me for the Fourth of July holiday weekend, just him and me in my family cabin. It would be his first time at our cabin and my first time inviting someone like him to our cabin, but he didn't know that. I had felt it was time, now that we had been dating for just under a year, to be able to share this part of my childhood with him. He was expected about an hour ago, but I just assumed he was running late after hitting traffic. I reached for my phone, which had been turned over to force me to ignore any distractions while I wrote. When I flipped it over, it lit up with over forty notifications, all from him.

Between missed calls, voicemails, and text messages, I learned he was lost somewhere in town. I call him.

"Hey baby, I'm so sorry I had my phone on silent," I say, "where are you? I'll come get you."

His tone was solid but soft, "I'm at a coffee shop in town; I'll send you my location," he responded.

It was midday, and I knew he was tired from his drive and would want to sleep once he got here. I told him I was on my way and I walked straight to my car, making sure my keys were in my pants pocket and neglecting putting any of my stuff away in the house safely.

The main area of town was about a thirty-minute drive, and when I arrived, it didn't take much time to find him. We were on a mission, so I didn't think to get out and hug him. Instead, I pulled up behind his car on the side of the road, he had parallel parked directly in front of the coffee shop on Main Street, and sent him a text that read: I'm here, do you want to just follow me home?

I watched from the driver's seat as he pushed open the door to the coffee shop, laptop, and coffee in hand, and smiled at me briefly.

I saw him as he gently laid his things in his seat, and he walked over to my driver's seat, pointing his finger to prompt me to roll the window down.

"Hey baby," he said, leaning in for a kiss "yeah, I'll just follow you" I respond with a nod of my head and watch him walk back to his car, careful again to move his possessions into the cup holder and passenger seat beside him.

I took that as my cue, and I turned my wheel to pull out in front of him so he could follow me home.

When we arrived, I got out of the car and guided him into his spot. I heard his engine sputter out, and I reached to open his driver's side door.

"I am so sorry," I said, reaching for his hand. He stepped out of the car and hugged me. We stood there for a minute, his car beeping incessantly from his door still being open, until he pulled away.

"This is beautiful, Eli. I'm excited," he said and turned to look at the house. He walked around the back of his car to get his belongings, and I closed his door with care before helping him with his bags. When we stepped inside, he took his shoes off, and I led him into our room for the next two nights.

I urged him to sleep, but he insisted against it, pulling me onto the bed and wrapping me in his arms.

"I don't want to miss out on this moment to be with you," he said. When he spoke like this, all of my worries melted away. All of my insecurities, my fears, and even my thoughts, ceased to exist.

"What're we doing tonight?" he asked, turning me on my back and looking down at me.

"Well, I thought we could go to the beach tonight and watch the stars. Then tomorrow morning, we can go into town. I have a few places I want to show you," he smiled, and I knew that was enough of an answer. I silently admired his ability to accept even the littlest of responses as if they were the most precious drops of knowledge dripping onto his tongue.

He lingered above me for a few moments before resting his head down on my chest. I moved my fingers through his hair and down his back, tracing the bumps of his spine as he went. The room was warm, not uncomfortably so, but noticeable because of our body heat. He looked back at me, now resting his chin on my chest, his eyes having to look upward at mine. I adjusted my head, aware that his view of me might be less than appealing.

"What's wrong?" he said, pulling his hand from underneath him and lifting himself up to get a better view of my face.

"Nothing," I said, confused.

"You look sad," he said and leaned in for a kiss.

I was not sad, but his question made me wonder whether or not I actually should be. Why did someone else get to decide for me how I was feeling at that moment? A question, I can understand, but to tell me I look sad? The fears and insecurities flooded back in and I wondered what I had done wrong to make him think such a thing, to make him accuse me of such an emotion.

I spoke nothing more and instead pushed him onto his back, taking off all of his clothes from him and tossing them to the floor.

Seconds later, I had him inside me. He smelled of laundry detergent and tasted of sweat and cheap cologne. It had become my favorite taste.

I performed more vigorously than I had ever done before and after only a few minutes, I could feel his entire body tense and he gripped my forearm with his right hand. Our other hands, intertwined, grasped each other tighter.

He throbbed in my mouth, and I knew what to expect. In multiple pulses, my mouth was filled with a salty wave of him that I quickly took as a reward for my work.

It wasn't until I heard him say, in a voice absent of power, "I think you've got it all" that I lifted my head and saw him, beads of sweat pilling on his face. His hands still gripped the sheets, almost in anticipation of anything that might come next. There was nothing left to do.

We lay there, both of us breathless, enjoying the moment. I could feel his heartbeat in his stomach, where my head now rested. His eyes were closed, and I didn't think to disturb him, so I closed mine as well, readjusting myself to a more comfortable position. My back was toward the doors that led outside, and at our feet were to the door that led out into the hallway.

He mumbled, "Thank you," and those were the last words I remember before I drifted off into a deep sleep.

I woke to a sound from behind me. He still slept softly under me, so I rolled off slowly and without a sound to investigate. The sun was beginning to set, so it was difficult to see outside. I opened one of the doors to the outside, my grip firm on the handle, and pushed. I peeked my head out and looked around. Nothing.

I took a step onto the deck and looked again. Suddenly, the flood light switched on.

"Eli?" a voice came from the door to the living room and kitchen. I turned to look and saw Pat, our family friend from town, looking back at me, confused.

"Oh, hi Pat. I'm here for the weekend with a friend." I told half the truth, not feeling comfortable sharing all of my business just because she had been a friend of the family.

"Eli, oh my goodness! It is good to see you. Your parents didn't mention anyone was going to be here this weekend; I just came over to check on the house. There were a few things left on the table out here that I brought inside; I'm assuming they are yours?" she said, and I nodded, remembering the laptop and glasses I had left earlier.

"Yeah, thank you, Pat. It is good to see you. If it has been a hassle, please stay for the evening. You're welcome for as long as you need." It felt odd to act like an adult, even though I knew I was one. Or perhaps this wasn't so much acting and something that anyone should be capable of doing. Should it come easily? *It would if he were awake, here with me.*

She smiled and stepped outside with me, and I realized I had lingered right outside my door as well. I closed it behind me, not wanting to disturb his sleep.

"Oh, stop it, I won't impose on your weekend with your friend. I'll just grab my things and be out of your hair. You enjoy yourselves, now," she responded; her thick accent made it difficult to understand her well. She was an Irishwoman. She and her husband moved into town when their son got a job in the big city. He and his new wife moved with their newborn daughter, and Pat thought it the perfect opportunity to uproot her life for her child.

I smiled at her as she walked back into the house. I opened the door again to my bedroom and backed inside.

The light was on, and the bed was empty. I opened the door to the hallway and saw the light in the bathroom on and shuffling from the kitchen. Settling into knowing that He was safe from Pat in the bathroom, I laid back down on the bed to wait for him.

I waited for thirty minutes before thinking about checking on Him. I got up and walked into the hallway, the entire house now illuminated in light. Homes away from town, covered by thick woods, and far from any other house always felt different at night. It made you feel as though you were the only one on the earth, almost like you were surviving off the land in some ignorant way. The darkness outside encouraged this feeling, levitating the house into an oblivion of sorts. Like, as the sun escaped and the moon rose, the home entered a portal to another dimension in which it and its inhabitants were the only living things. Houses were living, too, because of the people that inhabited them.

He was sitting at the kitchen island, looking at me with a smile on his face.

"Sleep well?" he said, his smile changing slightly to show the teeth on the left side of his mouth. He had changed into a different set of clothes, bundling up with a hoodie and a denim jacket over it.

"I was waiting for you; I thought you had just gone to the bathroom," I said, walking up to him. I put my hands on his cheeks, and he pulled away slightly.

"Your hands are cold," he grabbed them in his own and rubbed them together.

"I made sandwiches for the beach. I hope that's okay," he said, nodding his head to the other side of the island where two Ziplock bags held the sandwiches in question.

I pushed against him, feeling his lips against my own.

"God, I love you" and I kissed him. He had never been here and he had made the place his own, not because he was inconsiderate but because he was caring. I felt his love in these moments.

We decided to take his car to the beach, it was his father's, and it was fortunate that it also happened to be the only 4WD car we had with us. We could've just walked down to the beach, but I knew I would get cold and I didn't know how long we would be out, so I figured this would be better.

He drove carefully onto the beach. I advised him on where to take the car and where not to, avoiding large mounds of loose, dry sand. He looked at me with his chocolate eyes, and I took mental note of how they looked in the moonlight. *I will never forget this*, I thought.

The car rolled into place onto the wet sand; the tide was all the way out, but I knew we'd have to keep an eye on the waves. I rolled the window down, and the wind immediately swept up my hair and pulled it in every direction. I reached up to fix it.

"I wish we could see the stars better from here," I said. The car was a sedan, but it was missing its sunroof, so the ugly gray-felt ceiling blocked our chance at an impeccable and warm view.

"Well, let's change that" he replied, opening the driver's side door. I followed his lead hesitantly and watched inquisitively as he lifted himself off the ground using the frame of the car and hoisting himself up onto the roof. I pulled myself out as well from the passenger side, standing on the frame of the car and watching him as he repositioned himself, sitting crisscross on the metal.

"You coming?" he said, looking down at me with a smile. The wind was lighter now but it still blew his hair askew. I was never a fan of any form of physical exercise and this is something that I considered physical exercise. Any opportunity for me to potentially embarrass myself, an opportunity that leaves room for error, is not an opportunity I want to take.

He noticed my discomfort and leaned closer to me, shifting his butt across the metal roof.

"Just step on the top of the tire there," he instructed, and I followed, "and then lift that leg on top of the hood," Again, I followed his instruction, "And then you can just crawl up, try not to put too much weight on the glass."

I maneuvered myself with as much grace as I could muster onto the roof of the car and spun myself around, dangling my feet off of the right side of the car momentarily before letting them rest over the glass on the front windshield. He was back into his crisscross position.

"This is a better view, I gotta admit," I said, and he laughed.

"Worth the hassle?" he joked, and I nudged him instinctively. It was a good opportunity for me to get closer to him, so I took it, edging myself closer so that our hip bones were touching in the center of the car. I reached my arm behind him and pulled him closer still, hooking my finger around the loop in his jeans. I use my other hand and place it behind me to steady myself. My head falls onto his right shoulder, and I nestle in as deep as I can.

"Definitely worth the hassle," even though I know he is already looking, I say, "look at the sky! You'd never see those stars in the city."

He doesn't say anything. I scan the black sky for any semblance of a star or grouping of stars I may recognize, landing my gaze on the big dipper. The moon lights up a small part of its surrounding area with a blue glow, like a flashlight dimmed by a child's hand, smushing the light and spreading it across a smaller space.

I can feel him smile above me. I move my head to watch him. His eyes are on the ocean. The waves are calm now, moving in at such a slow rate it is impossible to even notice.

His eyes glint in the moonlight. "Hey," I start, "I really love you." he looks over at me, his smile unchanging.

"I love you, too. You know that." he says, leaning in for a kiss. His lips are warm but salty with the ocean's mist. *He didn't understand what I was trying to say.*

How do you utter words of love to someone without saying those three words? How does someone express something deeper than love; is there a feeling more complex than love?

I try again. "What I mean is you really mean a lot to me, like I can't express it well enough in words."

"You explained it just fine," he said, keeping eye contact with me. I knew he didn't understand the impact of his words, but they stung against my ears.

"Okay, good," I said, and then silence. The only sound were the waves crashing in front of us. We both turned our gaze back, me to the sky and him to the ocean. The sky was vast and unknown, but then again so was the ocean. We had more answers for the sky, though, and I thought about the mystery and fear that might exist in the ocean was enough to dissuade me from thinking about it.

"Do you think we will last?" I said, finally. I don't know what compelled me to say it, maybe the thought of the vast unknown of our relationship. The sky and the ocean combined had more answers than the future of love.

He stays quiet for a moment, and I think he must be processing the question and navigating the perfect response. Then, the silence lingers, and my fear begins to creep in. This is one of the first times where I feel an anxiety like this around him.

"I don't know," he says finally, and I wish he had lied.

That is the answer, though, and the most honest one.

"If you don't, who does? If you ask me, I would say yes." I say, hoping to spark a conversation. It was also true, though, that we are the ones that decide what happens, how everything will work out.

"I think you think too much. All these questions, we can't answer. It's better not to answer because, ultimately, we have to know we can't." The freckle on his upper lip became the focal point of my view. I didn't dare raise my glance to his.

I thought about his words. They pierced my skin and entered every cell, trying to escape again by pushing goose bumps out from my skin. They couldn't escape, and so they poisoned every nerve and vein in my body, entering my soul. *Was he right?* It would be better to just accept that nothing past this moment right here has any significance. And, even if it did, could we control it? Or was that for a being higher than us to answer and in giving us the ability to question it, that being must laugh at our futile and fruitless attempt.

"All I mean is," he grabs my hand, "we are here, now. And everything is good. Let it just be good" he presses my hand against his lips and I can feel a tear begin to form in my eye.

Suddenly, my entire body drops two inches closer to the earth, and I fall into him. The metal of the roof caved in from our weight, and I immediately jumped from the car, embarrassed.

"It's okay, it's okay!" he says, and gently climbs off the top, "this has happened before," he reaches into the car through the driver's side and with one swift push, the dent resolves.

When had this happened before?

The next day, we woke late. I had made sure to cover the window and glass doors from the morning sun the night before. After letting the sleep slowly wash from our eyes, we leisurely ate breakfast and got ready for the day. It was my turn to drive, so we packed our day bags and got into the car. I turned the heat to the highest setting and rubbed my hands together, trying to eradicate the cold from them. We sat in silence as I drove. He played music, somber songs, from one of his favorite musicals. He had slipped in a few of my indie rock songs that were a bit upbeat.

On the agenda for the day: antique store, Book store, lunch, and home. It was a perfect date, one I knew he would love and one that incorporated both of our favorite things.

We pull into our parking spot and he reaches for my hand.

"Thank you for planning today," he said

"Of course. I'm sorry for last night," I say, pushing open the driver's side door and stepping out onto the wet asphalt before he has a chance to respond.

The day is cold, and the sun is almost at its peak in the sky. A brisk wind presses against my skin, and I swear I can feel the mist from the sea dampening it.

As we walked, I felt his hand brush up next to mine. His movement was awkward, so I closed the gap and grabbed his fingers, interlocking them with my own. Electricity surged through me, and the tension eased.

The door was open as we approached the antique store. It was a large warehouse placed between two undisclosed corporate buildings. It was out of place, but most good antique stores are nowadays. The sign, ANTIQUE GOODS, was lit up in large block letters above the massive sliding metal door. As we entered, we were affronted by the smell of mildew and dust—arguably the best smell, second to old books.

It was quiet, the only sound coming from the shuffling feet of the few people who walked around us. The aisleways were narrow, packed high with old belongings of those forgotten, or just simply belongings forgotten by those who no longer knew, or cared to know, how to care for them anymore. It seemed to go on forever, and there were a set of wooden stairs leading up to the second floor.

"Look at how cute these are" he said, walking swiftly up to a small paper nail box. I was expecting to see nails but instead, inside were hundreds of small antique skeleton keys. I looked at them, reached in and grabbed one, and pulled it up into the light. It was small, silver, and yet still heavy. I wondered who would have owned something like this, and to which lock would it belong.

He rubbed my back gently, putting enough pressure so as to reach me through my jacket and shirt, and then moved on.

I trailed behind him closely, pocketing the key slyly.

I watched him pensively the entire time, taking note of the things he looked at for longer than a few seconds, wondering what he may be thinking. We walked in silence all the way up until the time we exited, the sun shining more brightly now- the wind moving with less vigor than before.

"I got this for you," I said, pulling the key from my back pocket.

"You stole it?" he said, pushing my hand back down from where it was, holding the key high for anyone to see.

"I saw you looking at it. It was only fifty cents, anyway," I replied, and my stomach began to bubble with embarrassment.

"Still," he said, but he grabbed it from me quickly and put it in his pocket, "Thank you."

As we walked to the bookstore, we discussed the weather, how the night before left us with a bit of scratchiness in our noses and throats, and the need for hot tea or cocoa soon.

"I have an idea," he spoke with enthusiasm as we approached the front door to the bookstore, "why don't we split up. You get a book you think I would like and I'll get one I think you would like."

I liked the idea and agreed, holding the door open for him and smiling as he passed by me. I could smell him as he passed, a warm and dark scent that left me with tingles throughout my skin. My mind began to race as I followed him into the store, thinking about all of the options of books I could choose for him.

The store was an old one, three stories, like a tenement building that had been gutted and replaced with rows and rows of bookshelves that stood twenty feet tall, stacked to the top with books of all different heights and widths.

It smelled similarly to the antique store, with incense burning in the corner and the resident tabby cat stretching out on the carpeted floor. I knew I wanted to explore each floor, even though the book I wanted to get for him was on the first.

They had everything; old books were further up whereas the newer selection and current best sellers sat on display on and around the tables that were delicately placed on the first floor.

A woman approached me as I took my last step onto the third floor. "May I help you?" she asked. She was a stout woman; curly reddish-brown hair covered her face. She readjusted her posture and moved the hair from her eyes. They were milky brown, almost eerily so, and they shined bright under the fluorescent lights. There was something mystical about her, the way she looked or the way she held herself. After repositioning her body, I could see her nametag more clearly; Andrea, it read, and I smiled.

"Yes, actually. I know it's a stretch, but I am wondering if you might have some older editions of this book that I'm looking for" I pulled my phone from my pocket and showed her a picture, "if you have this cover art, too, that would be even better" she looked at the picture and smiled, like she already knew what book I was looking for.

"This way," she said, and walked toward the back of the floor. I had accepted that it would be alright if I found a newer version of the book on the first floor, but now my heart fluttered with excitement at the idea of there possibly being an older edition.

"Looks like you're in luck" she said, and pointed to a row of books on the bottom shelf in the very far aisle of the floor. All of them were varying sizes and colors, each with their own unique and distinct mark of wear on them.

I reached down to grab one and as I stood, I turned to say thank you, but Andrea was gone. I turn back to the book, not thinking much of it, and open the cover to see the information on the inside.

First Edition Print reads in small typewriter letters.

Holy shit, I think, and look around to see if anyone is watching me. It's that odd feeling everyone gets, thinking someone is watching you when you happen upon something like this. It's almost like someone should be watching you in order to make it real. In order to make it important.

I run back downstairs and check out, making sure he doesn't see me as I do.

I wait for him outside. I watch from the cold as he checks out and walks to leave the store, clutching his own brown paper bag that holds my book in it.

"This was a good idea," I say, as the door swings closed behind him.

"Thank you," he responded with a kiss to my forehead, "do you want to grab lunch on the way home and exchange once we're back?" I smile, shifting the bag from my right hand to my left and grabbing his hand, gripping it tightly.

When we arrived back at the cabin, I couldn't contain my excitement.

"Let's eat first," he said, putting our food down on the kitchen counter. I audibly sighed and leaned into him, and he unloaded the food. We had opted for a local sandwich shop; we had both gotten a soup and sandwich combo. My stomach grumbled at the smell of the warm food wafting up from its brown bag, but I still wanted to open the book first. I couldn't tell what I was more excited for; seeing him open his book, his favorite book in a first edition worth God knows how much, or seeing what book he chose for me.

I reached my arms around him from behind, turning him quickly to hug him from the front. We stood in the kitchen; his backside was against the kitchen counter where the food sat. My arms were mid-level against his back; I could feel his muscles tense and loosen at my touch. He put his arms around me and we stood there, tightly encased in our own bubble, for minutes on end.

After what felt like over five minutes, He whispered in my ear, "Is everything okay?"

I smiled and hugged him tighter. A feeling of uneasiness spread over me, ruining the beautiful moment. I tried to push the paranoia from my mind.

"Everything is fine," I mumbled back, "it's just…" I could feel his chest puff up, and he exhaled a long, breathy sigh into my ear.

"Why does it feel like this will be the last time I get to feel you against me?" I said, regretting it almost immediately.

He pulls away and looks at me wildly, confused. His reaction tells me I should never speak my true thoughts, let alone my true feelings. I need to be more calculated and more delicate.

"Why would you say something like that?" he exclaims.

"Forget it, let's eat." I say and then mumble an "I'm sorry" before reaching behind him to grab the food and bring it to the table.

We ate in what was becoming a familiar silence. I watched a spot on the window in the kitchen. It began to bother me.

We finished our food in an excruciatingly slow amount of time, but finally it was time for our books. It no longer held the same excitement for me, and he noticed, so he pulled me over to the couch in the living room. The fire was burning and I sat on the side closer to the fire.

"I'm not sure what's going on in your head," he began. *Nothing*, I thought, lying even to myself.

"But you know I love you." he kneeled in front of me, spreading my legs and nestling between them. He put his head on the zipper of my jeans, and I felt a surge of excitement run through me. *Why, during a serious moment, would my body betray me in such a way.*

"So… Can I open mine first?" He said, reaching for the paper bag he had brought over from the kitchen. I nodded solemnly and put my hand on his leg as he sat beside me, so close he was almost sitting on me. I watched as he delicately unraveled the paper and peered inside. I wished he would just rip it open instead of being so careful.

He pulls out the book; paperback, weathered but still in an okay condition with a few tears on the top, the pages browned from age.

"Eli," he whispered. I looked at him, but he couldn't meet my gaze. Tears began to well in his eyes, and one began to fall from his face. I watched as it trickled down, following the natural contour of his laugh lines. I lifted my hand up and wiped it away.

"It's a first edition," I said, kissing his cheek. Another tear fell, and then another, until he was a mess in front of me. I held him as he sobbed against me, the book still in his hand.

We spent the rest of the evening at each other's side in silence. That night, I didn't open my book. But when I did, it was a copy of his favorite book- of which I already had three.

CHAPTER ELEVEN

When the World Ends

Something in my new that, on my drive home, separate from him, would be the last time.

I felt a tinge of the stranger entering my body, that feeling that causes a seemingly unending disillusionment and dissociation. It was coming more frequently now, that he was gone. It passes, as they always do, and I feel gutted once more, another piece of myself lost to the unknown.

The stranger, what I've now named it, was the thing that crept in through all the major events of my life. And with each one, a piece of myself was torn and taken, leaving me feeling like an imposter within my own school. These things that happened to me, Him leaving me, all forced me to realize that the life I was living was nothing special. That I was not immune to the consequences of man.

I'm driving back down the interstate, back to the eerie comfort of home, the world I always lived in and knew I could go back to. As I pass cars on my right, I think about the lives of those within them, if they feel that some part of them have been stripped as well at some point or by someone.

The window, now rolled down, offers a slap of reality as the wind whips the seatbelt back and forth. I press the buttons for all the windows, allowing the air to move more freely.

What is a legacy if it's already been left by someone before? I think to myself.

Surely someone before me, someone at this very moment, and someone in the near and far future will do exactly as I am doing- roll their windows down, stick their arms out, and ride the waves with their hand against the whipping wind. And yet, I still feel that somehow, my doing it matters. Or, at the very least, it has meaning to me. Is that enough?

My mind floods with thoughts that I disdain and so, wishing to force them all down, I roll the windows back up and put both of my hands on the wheel. I feel like I'm being watched. Someone, the stranger maybe, is laughing at the way I am acting, entering into my mind and smirking at the way my thoughts wander to unforgiving places.

As I drive, I feel pieces of myself break away and dissolve into dust, memories floating in the air and out of sight. *This can't be it,* I think. I roll the windows back down and turn the music higher than the car can handle. Now, even the world seems to be breaking apart before me, and I am nothing. I have no power to stand in its way.

My body begins to shake, and every thought, every feeling, ejects itself from my body in a torrent of tears and violent shakes. My vision blurs as I wipe frantically at my face, trying to maintain vision on the road, wishing still to stand witness to the destruction of my life.

This continues for some time. I don't remember getting home, finding my way to my room in the darkness, and crawling into bed for a demanded sleep. But, even without my knowing, the process of my undoing had already begun years ago, and it had finally reached its conclusion.

CHAPTER TWELVE

A Trip Cut Short... Again

My brain freezes, but my body jumps into action. I am running past the three of them, Diana, Hudson, and Him. The wind is now whipping against my face, and I have no time to process the implications of my action, the way they may be interpreting my running from them in such a way. The waves to my right lap more rigorously against the sand than before. I don't stop. I know they are behind me, watching me as I run, but I don't stop.

I reach the steps of the cabin and fall to the ground to catch my breath. The cool air feels good against my skin. My shirt clings to my back from sweat, and I shiver as a gust of wind turns the wetness to ice. My hands are against the dark earth, a patch where the grass has not grown, and the dirt has turned muddy from the moisture in the air. I push in deeper, letting the tips of my fingers disappear beneath the ground. I sit like this for a long time, my hands in the earth, breathing heavily from running.

I hear steps from behind me.

"Eli, just talk to me." He was behind me, close now but still a few hundred yards behind on the path. *How much time had passed?* I pull myself up, clapping my hands together as I ascend the steps and pull open the doors to the living room of the cabin, wanting so badly to slam them closed behind me.

The house had a different feel to it now, almost as if it was actively pushing me out or wanting me to leave. Like it knew what I had done, and it was disappointed in me and didn't want me to feel at home any longer. I think to stomp all the way to my bedroom but I stop and spin around to face him. My eyes fall to the floor. I fixate on the spot where, years ago, someone had dropped a knife in the floor, leaving a perfectly clean slice in the now-weathered hardwood. I still remember how mad my mom had been when that happened.

"Listen, Hudson, I've done it all, I've grown, I've learned, I've experienced. I don't need to speak my mind anymore; I don't need to put my painful thoughts into the world." I looked at him. His eyes were already swelling with tears, the white of his eyes blood shot. *Why was he crying?* I thought, wanting so badly to ask him.

"But do you know what to do with those thoughts, Eli?" he says, "if you don't put them into the world. If you don't speak them out loud, if not to everyone, at least to someone, what are you doing with them?"

"What would be the point?" I say, a tear falling from my face. The first, it seems, in years. My face flushes red with embarrassment, or anger, or a mix of the two I didn't really know.

"Look, I get it, okay?" I was breathing heavily, my chest rising at an unnatural rate, "everyone wants to feel like they are doing the right thing and they are living a life that is different, but if they just took a step back from that and maybe realize that life isn't so much of a fantasy that they want it to be, their lives would actually feel some version of fulfillment. It isn't in talking about our feelings that we suddenly find purpose." I say, throwing my hands up. My breath had been exhausted, and I faltered on the last few words.

Hudson huffed. I felt compelled to continue.

"Why do you care so much, anyway?" I say, attempting to speak as softly as I can so as not to sound harsh or accusatory. I don't think it has fully clicked yet for him, but it didn't really need to. The air in the room felt cool against my skin, and I felt myself wishing I could sit.

"I know you expect me to say some profound thing, but I can't, okay?" I said, willing the tears to stop flowing.

He looked at me intensely, and I could tell from his expression that he was working out a way to respond to me. His face contorted in a way I hadn't seen before.

"You will never get it, will you?" he said, his tone was angry, one I had not seen from him yet in the short time I have known him. He turned and began to walk away from me. I felt that he expected me to follow after him, but there wouldn't be much point. If I continued this game, neither one of us would come out unbruised, either in ego or otherwise.

I took my chance to sit at the living room table, in the same chair he had sat in when we first arrived. His book was still lying open, upside down, so I could see both the front and back covers. The spine had been broken, so it lay almost entirely flat against the wood. I took this opportunity to look at the title, East of Eden, by John Steinbeck. It had been a book I'd put on my reading list for years but had never gotten around to. Surprising now as I realized that Hudson was probably reading it because it was his brother's favorite. I picked it up, turning through the thin pages and wondering if it was his brother's original copy. Hudson had left the room, and yet my heartbeat continued at a fast pace. *Where was Diana?* In the chaos, I hadn't even thought about where she, or He, might have been or done when I stormed away. The sun had almost entirely risen in the sky, shining in through the windows and casting a bright flow on the table and floor. We hadn't determined a set day to leave, though it was clear our trip had met its end.

I wasn't quite sure where he had gone, Hudson, but I stayed seated and looked out the window for any sign of Diana. It wasn't until about twenty minutes of silence that I saw her walking back up the wooden steps and onto the back porch up to the front door. Her feet pressed gently against the wood, and no sound came from them except for the faint creak. As she walked, the footprints from her sneakers left a dewy and sandy remnant behind.

She opened the door, and her expression was wild; it didn't match her movements at all. She moved gracefully towards the table where I sat, not even bothering to remove her shoes in the process, which tracked sand from the beach all the way to the place across from me. She didn't speak. Instead, she just sat quietly and looked at me, a wild look in her eyes. It wasn't fear, I knew that much for sure, though I couldn't quite place it.

"What was that?" she put her hands flat on the bench, lifting herself and leaning forward with her breasts against the table. Still, in her dress, she looked out of place here in the living room.

"I'm leaving today. This trip was a mistake." I say and without thinking, I place the book back down on the table, the page Hudson was on disappears in the folds of the pages as they close into each other.

Diana rolls her eyes, "okay, where is Hudson?" She stands now, looking around. I don't respond and she walks away from me, towards the direction of his room.

I wait, the bench hard beneath me, and invite the noise of silence. I allow it to fill my ears, to deafen me.

Some time passed, and Diana and Hudson reentered my space. Diana looked briefly at me with a gentle look in her eyes before passing me and stepping outside. Hudson, however, sat across from me.

They had put the pieces of the puzzle together with their stories; I could just tell.

"I'm leaving," I say before he gets a chance to speak. He smiles at me, and my body shivers. His is the same as his brothers, as I'm just noticing now, small and perfect, with a lift on one end.

"Small world," he says, lifting his hands to his face. He smooths out the lines on his face with his hands, pushing away the expression of confusion with it. "What you don't understand, Eli, is that you are allowed to feel. Whatever you're battling, you can battle with me."

The innocent look on his face disturbed me. He doesn't understand, he couldn't. I think, for a moment, about the childhood I lost from Him. And here Hudson was, His own brother, trying to tell me that I can trust him?

It surged through me like the intensity of medicine entering your veins through the needle. I was like a surge of electricity coursing through every inch of my body, trying to find an exit point and failing. My blood and skin seem to tingle with its abruptness. Was it me? The thought that so often was a fleeting one filled me and formed solid against every crevice of my body and mind. It stuck.

Is it me? No, it couldn't be. Why do I have to accept love again? Why do I have to admit vulnerability? It's not real.

I understand that life is worth living, so don't doubt me about that. I know Hudson, still sitting across from me with his eyes wanting, is expecting an answer. What he doesn't seem to understand is how finite life is. Everyone searches for a way in which to immortalize themself, and I value their vigor. Although, I also question it. I question their ability to remain ignorant even in the face of truth, the face of what's real amongst the fake. It is what his brother so easily did, accept ignorance, and now what Hudson was doing. And I couldn't allow myself to fall into the same trap. I had allowed these experiences to dictate how I am in my adult life, and I am better off for it. *Aren't I?* Growing up is realizing that your childhood self can never just stay a child but becomes you as you transition to adulthood.

"I can appreciate what you're trying to do, Hudson, I do. But you don't know what he did to me. You don't know the lessons he taught me," I say finally. I can feel a tear begin to swell in my eyes again, giving me goosebumps. I look down at my arms and see them prickly and numerous. Each bump is like a memory of my past, a jerk and instinctive reaction in my body trying to convince me that there are still moments of awe and genuine beauty. Or is it simply a trick of the mind, an attempt of the brain to get me to feel… something? I can't think of the last time I got goosebumps from something other than the cold. More than a feeling of vulnerability, I felt embarrassed that my body was betraying me, showing something to the world that had no right to be seen. Every word I say stabs deeper into me, every instinct willing me to stop.

"And I don't need to know, Eli, if you don't want to tell me. But, respectfully, cut the bullshit. I hate that you don't care about anything."

"I care too much!" I say, "That's the problem, Hudson, don't you get that?" I hold the tears in. "It only hurts me to care, and why would anyone want to willingly allow themselves to hurt? So, I learned how to eliminate that part of me, accept reality, and allow life to just run its course. Feelings, actions, and anything else will just come and pass, and we have no control over them. So, I took control of what I did have power over." I say, thinking to add *you're only purpose in life is to find no purpose. It's just to simply exist. Existing isn't something that we can control. Death we can control, life we can control, but existence- that's what we must all work toward*, but decide against it.

"You can't control me, Eli." he says.

"Isn't that the point I am trying to make, Hudson? I don't want to control you or influence you. When I think something and only think it, everything is fine and well, but the moment I speak it into existence, you would latch onto every word, its every sound, my every utterance, and corrupt it. Why put either of us through the hassle?"

"Because what other choice do we have but to try?" he says, his voice louder than before. I can tell he is scared of something, but he masks it well with his anger.

"Can't we just accept that to exist, to live, and to die are all beautiful things, but to learn, to engage, to communicate- that is where life truly matters. You're living in a limbo, Eli." he pauses to wipe a tear from his face. He looks out the window. I follow his gaze to see Diana on the phone.

"Let people like him live the way they want to live, but don't let it decide how to live your life or how to treat others who live theirs differently" he speaks to me but not at me.

What was he asking of me, and why? If I agree or admit to this, am I betraying Him? Or am I betraying myself? Does growing mean forgetting the past?

Then, fear overtakes my entire body. *If Hudson made it here behind me, would He be trailing closely behind, with Diana?*

I look at Hudson directly into his eyes and speak clearly.

"I don't want him in my house," I said, turning away from him and toward my bedroom to collect my things. As I walked, I shivered at the thought of his eyes, so cruelly similar to his brothers: gentle yet bright. *How did I not notice it before?*

IV.

THE END

No Care in the World

CHAPTER ONE
Lesson Learned

I remained in my room until nightfall, until I figured there would be no reason for the coast not to be clear. Hudson and his brother would have left by now, knowing full well they were not welcome, and Diana would want to speak with me. I dreaded that conversation but knew it needed to happen. I needed to go, back to New York, or to someplace else. This trip, I was realizing, had caused too much turmoil for me in just a few short days. I took a moment to look out to the trees from the double doors in my room.

I search them, now overcast by the falling sun, for an inch of color that I know existed just moments before. And there is none. They are black or void of color, I suppose. From the tips of their leaves to the bark that their limbs grow from. They sway back and forth as if still asking for attention, but the sunset steals it. I wonder if that's what it's like to lose yourself, to be like the trees in a world of sunsets. Or maybe the tree hasn't lost itself, maybe its color is still there even though it can't be seen. Perhaps it's been reimagined, reawakened in the birth of a new night with each turn of the sun. Life, too, then, may be reimagined behind its meaninglessness, its distraction, its noise.

When I emerged, a single light was on in the living room. There was silence, a silence I had never known before, and as I walked into the living room, I realized that the single light was not even a light at all. The light from Hudson's phone screen lit up the darkness, illuminating his face in an almost creepy glow. As I approached, he raised his head to look at me. The light cast a shadow against his face that was not appealing in the slightest.

"I thought maybe you'd escaped out the door to your bedroom or something," he said, a grim smile spreading across his face. I walked over to the light switch and lifted my hand, wanting to flip it when he stopped me.

"Don't, please," he said, and as my eyes began to adjust to the darkness, I could see him motioning for me to sit down beside him. In the absence of light, the darkness always seems to find some way to vastly illuminate even the tiniest slivers of its counterpart. As such, the moon shone through the kitchen windows.

I sit at the table, and as I do, I wonder where Diana must have gone. On cue, like he always had before, he answers the question I am thinking in my mind.

"I asked Diana to go into town. She's dealing with her own stuff, you know." he says in an accusatory manner, and I wondered if she and him had spoken about her divorce. What did I not know?

"She decided to stay the night in town," he began, lifting his hands to his face and rubbing the sleep from his eyes. He stands, grabs a bottle of wine and two glasses from the cupboards, and walks back to sit down beside me. I listen intently to the sound of the liquid filling each glass.

"She's a good woman, your sister," he says, placing the bottle back down on the table and pushing a glass toward me. I wince at his words, at the thought that this man, who is still a stranger to me, could potentially know more about my sister than her own sibling.

"I need to explain something to you, Eli," he begins again, and I realize he is struggling to find the words, "I know you don't want me here, and I have been beating myself up all day wondering how I couldn't have known who you were to my brother, or even who my brother was to you. I guess we don't know the people we are supposed to know most almost as much as we like to think we do." he swishes his glass around, deep in thought, "Anyway, he told me everything. You meant a lot to him," he said, breathing in deeply.

I take a long gulp of my glass. How could I have meant a lot to him if he left me? After everything, he just left me. Hudson's words sting, but I know that they are coated in what was a fabricated story through the eyes of his brother. I'll accept his ignorance in not being able to identify that.

"It's clear, now, that any relationship that I dreamed of with my brother when I was a kid is no longer realistic for me. And I am assuming the same may be true for your sister?" he asked the question but continued as if he already knew the answer was yes.

"I was hoping to surprise my brother with a trip. That isn't going to happen anymore, and I think it is better deserved for someone else, anyway."

I respond, still holding my glass of wine, "Why is that not going to happen anymore?" I said, and he shook his head, taking a long gulp from his wine.

"I think you and I both could go without talking about him anymore. Am I right about that?" I nodded.

"Good. So, I have two one-way tickets to Ireland. I want you to come with me, Eli." he said, and the sound of glass against the wooden table jolted me upright.

"Why would you want that?" I said out of instinct.

What was he not telling me? What did he and his brother talk about in my absence?

"You need something new. I realized I do, too," he said kindly.

My response was short and sharp, "But why with me?"

He sighed and looked at me. The moon reflected off his eyes, and my arms grew goosebumps at their familiarity. "Both of us, you and I, are the ones always cast aside. Don't you feel that way? Why don't we just take control, finally, and do something worth living for."

I laughed gently, but in the silence, it seemed to reverberate off of every object in the house. My face flushed with embarrassment.

"You and I, similar? No. What you don't seem to understand is that your brother, your flesh and blood, broke me. That was years ago and, of course, no longer worth talking about. But I rebuilt myself and, in doing so, accepted that life just happens. Work, buying a home, and relationships just happen to us. When we think we have control, that's when we lose." I pause for another sip of wine, "and the faster we realize that, the better. Your brother has known that for years, since before I knew him, I expect, and it's time you learn it, too."

We sit, then, in silence for a few moments. I've already said more than I've wanted to, but I continue. I am keenly aware of the lack of food in my stomach, which gives the wine too much power. I shift as I feel it trickle down and course throughout my veins.

"That's what he taught me. Take my sister, she thought she had done it all right. And look where she is now. She took control, and it cost her. Life will always win."

He poured himself another glass of wine. I think he enjoyed hearing me talk. Or maybe he was just processing the different ways he could argue with me.

"You, actually, are the only one that seems to have it all figured out. And you're telling me you don't have control? From the outside looking in, your lack of control is actually working out pretty well for you."

Now, he laughed.

"And I could say the same about you. You always know when to stay quiet and when to speak, and when you do, the profound words that come out of your mouth are ones anyone would be lucky to hear. Isn't that just it, then? You've accepted life hasn't mattered, I can't accept that- and yet we both feel that we have no control. So, what is the answer?"

I shake my head. He knows my answer is that there doesn't need to be an answer.

"The answer is us, Eli. The answer is in this conversation right here." he taps his finger on the table, trying to make his point more known. "You know, you've got this kind of superpower that I've never seen in anyone else. I don't know if anyone else in your life has noticed it, let alone mentioned it. But I'm determined to figure you out."

I looked at him, his eyes wet with tears. "What power is that? All I am is a single person saying and doing exactly what I need and want to say and do. There doesn't need to be any analysis of it."

"Look, you've made yourself clear, okay? I'm not welcome here anymore, and I'll respect that. You know I'm leaving in two days. If you choose to join me, your ticket is on the side table by the front door. All I will say is this; you say and do exactly as you feel. People don't have that luxury- they spend their entire lives trying to fake themselves just for the mere attempt at constructing a version of themselves that they want the world to see. You, though. Your superpower is that you don't fake your thoughts. You just conceal them better than anyone."

"If I don't, what happens then? If I don't, I lose power. What I say, the things I do, all of it will be used against me. They always have been."

"Well, Eli, maybe that's your Achilles heel, your flaw." he pauses, and I think he's about to stand and walk away without giving me another word. He continues, "But aren't you tired? Aren't you tired of thinking of every word to delicately string together to deliver the appropriate consequence? And even then, once that consequence has been carried out, what if it still doesn't go the way you planned? Then you've been proven weak, and your flaw is visible to the world. What then? Did you ever think that maybe your power could be this, right here, what we are doing now?" he raises his voice and stands, enunciating every word, "I mean, God, I've never seen you more real than you are right now!" with that he plops back down and lifts his glass to the ceiling, downing every last drop.

I don't need time to think; the wine is flowing heavily through me, my brain is flushing with heat, and the memories that have led me to this moment race through my mind and seem to exit from my mouth. I don't even have a chance to think before I say, "I don't even know who I am, Hudson. I never have! I've never felt more free than after completely being shattered by your brother. And it wasn't even him; it was my ignorance, my inability to see that I was weak, and giving myself away to someone when I didn't even have the right to give myself away."

My eyes are hot, either from lack of sleep or the emergence of tears, I cannot tell. But I don't care. I glare at him, daring him to respond.

He sighs loudly and puts his head on the table. From beneath, I hear him mumble.

"What did you just say?" I say, fire burning in my eyes.

He lifts his head and meets my gaze, "No one knows who they are and everyone gives themselves away. But this," he pauses briefly, "this version of you is the absence of all the other Eli's that live within you."

"I know that Eli lives in there, it's time to bring them out," he says with finality, and we both sit for a few moments, the silence overwhelming us and gripping tightly to our skin.

I try to find him in his eyes but only see his brother. The air seems to loosen, and the silence is a welcome relief. I missed Him.

Without thinking, I close the gap between us, placing my lips against his sloppily. I feel him push toward me, accepting the feeling of my skin against his. I'm not thinking, and maybe that's the point; perhaps that is what has brought us to this point. And maybe that's beautiful.

The kiss ends, and he pulls away. *I worry that he knows that wasn't for him, that it wasn't him I was kissing* but someone else. He stands and leaves me to my thoughts, a half-empty bottle of wine and two red-stained glasses.

CHAPTER TWO

The End

Two days have passed. It is the morning, and even with summer at our fingertips, I feel within my soul a deafening call for winter. While the grass fades to brown and the sun beats down on its inhabitants outside, the coldness within me radiates, though it doesn't evoke fear. No, it hasn't evoked fear in years. Instead, I feel calm. He is leaving today, and I will go with him. I've evolved into a being of knowledge and, therefore, of corruption and recognition that life thrives solely for those who exist in ignorance. Those who, unbeknownst to them, live in the darkness of light while the rest of us live explicitly in a space that is absent of light. But, in this absence of light in which few of us live, we understand the truth. So perhaps here, the line between light and dark is blurred; maybe we live in such an absence of light that, in fact, the world to us is even more illuminated.

Diana sits on the hood of the new rental car, biting her nails softly. We leave each other today, our own selves, and we put it all behind us to rebuild. I don't know if I will ever see her again, my sister, but it doesn't really matter. I hope she's learned something from this, and I hope she finds what she's looking for. Maybe I hope she's found the darkness that I found years ago. In that darkness, she would discover light.

I wonder what goes on in her mind right about my decision with Hudson. Does she think she's won, somehow? Does she think she was right? Or, I wonder, does she hope I break what she considers to be my darkness with him? I am intrigued by the thought, knowing that it must be fruitless to break the thing I have worked so hard to construct. Then, on the other hand, was it really my own construction or that of all the experiences I've had and the people I've met?

The car was coming to take me to Philadelphia and Diana would watch me go. Maybe for the last time.

"What are you going to do without me?" she says playfully, sliding off of the hood and pulling a cigarette from her pocket. She lights it in front of me and takes a long drag, exhaling a puff of smoke into the spring air.

"Taking up smoking again?" I respond, rolling my eyes, "I think I could ask you the same."

She laughs on impulse before taking another long drag, her eyes following the smoke as it dissipates in the air above us.

"I suppose I can do whatever I want, now. Is that the freedom you've always felt?" in her eyes I see something I haven't seen before, a flicker of realization and recognition like finally, she feels a familial connection to me.

"Freedom? Or incarceration? You've always seen me as limited by my mind- incapable in ways you never were. It just came easy to you, you know, making decisions" I grabbed the cigarette from her hand and pulled in a long drag.

She leaned back on the hood of the car, digging her shoes into the gravel driveway, kicking up some of the small rocks and displacing them, allowing the dirt to show.

"Look where that got me," she said and began building a mound of rocks between her feet.

"Thank you, Eli, for this," her hands fly up and she slaps them back down to her sides. I hand her back the cigarette and she flicks it to the ground, crunching it beneath her feet.

Just then, before I can respond, the car pulls into the driveway. The vehicle that will take me to my next adventure.

"Enjoy Hudson's car," I say, pulling her in for a hug, "and please, do something good in your life now. It's time" I whisper. I don't know why I feel compelled to say it, but that thought deserved a voice, and I don't know if it would have lived without me.

She doesn't say anything except squeeze me harder. I pull away and open the passenger side door, sliding in as the driver loads my small bag in the trunk. I refuse to turn my head, only daring to lay my gaze on the glistening glass of the windshield before me.

CHAPTER THREE

Backwards To Philly

The ride to the airport was long. The driver insisted on his music the entire way, stopping it only to take phone calls from family and friends, speaking in a language I didn't recognize. It felt uncomfortable, nonetheless, to be an idle bystander to a conversation of a complete stranger, so intimately involved but also so disconnected. It felt wrong, almost, even though I couldn't understand what was being said.

The car ride turned into a train ride, which blended in with the security line at the airport. It wasn't until I had reached the gate that I saw him.

He looked at me with his brown eyes, the whites around them beaming brightly at me even in the grossly lit airport, giving an eerie light to the darkened irises in the center. He didn't stand but instead moved his backpack, settled next to him, to the floor. I was expecting his surprise, at the very least, but nothing crossed his face save for a subtle and almost sad smile.

"I'm glad you came," he said with an attempt at sincerity. I could tell that something was wrong.

We were early, and there weren't many others sitting around us. Even still, the airport felt busy, people rolling their suitcases behind them, some in pajamas, others in formal attire. Families, no doubt heading to their next vacation, argued when the youngest dropped their bag to the crowd, leading to the entire unit falling apart. That familiar feeling, that tug at the back of my mind, pulled at me, leaving me with prickles against the back of my neck. *Where are they all going? I wonder. Where do all of their lives take them?*

"You were expecting your brother?" I say, realizing that my being here was a mistake. I sit beside him, pushing myself as far into the seat as I can. It's not too late to leave, I think, to return to what was before. At least I still have that choice.

I can tell by his silence that he is thinking of what to say. I know now that he may even be intimidated, afraid to say the wrong thing in front of me.

"Yes. But I also needed you here." I look at him, and I can't help but notice the curve of his cheekbones into his chin. He seems more and more like his brother.

I didn't want to care for him, but someone pulled me in, making me wonder what his mind was playing at. It is all a game.

I choose not to respond, unaware really of how to respond. *Did he think I came for him?*

"This will be good for both of us," he said, almost as if to convince himself as much as to convince me. I barely recognize that he's had a change of heart.

The truth is, I didn't need convincing. I didn't care enough to be convinced. But I nodded, giving him some comfort. That felt necessary, at least.

CHAPTER FOUR

Left Behind

And so, as I sit in the Philadelphia airport, Hudson is now beside me, chewing loudly on a bagel with cream cheese and slurping down a macchiato. I wonder if everything has brought me to this moment for a reason.

It's a freeing feeling, knowing that at my fingertips lay the world and a potential new life. Where here, I leave this life of Eli Greene in Philadelphia and explore what might come next. And, even more freeing, the idea that maybe that exploration would lead to nothing at all. Left behind with this past life, this fabrication of a life built on the experiences and people from my past is the stranger. Something known to us all, rearing its ugly head in infinite forms, will finally be left here unattached from my soul.

I don't even know how it had clung itself to me, or at what point it took control over my own mind, and it may take time for its effect to wear off. I look to Hudson and wonder where his stranger is, if it lives within him still or if he is leaving it behind with his brother. I can't ask.

In this life, I have, without knowledge, opened myself to the indifference of men, to those who took and take advantage, to the systems of the structured and civilized world, all for their gain and a loss of my freedom. To close myself was to maintain my freedom. But now, it is clear that indifference to the world begs for my willingness and vulnerability because regardless of what it may do with me, it is only in that that there is freedom. And I will welcome it gladly.

CREDITS

"Liberation comes only when one understands that their life has already been lived before."

This book follows Eli Greene, a self-proclaimed expert on everything involving life, through a journey of life's many experiences. There are lessons to be learned and feelings to be familiarized with and mastered, and Eli walks us through the simplicity of it all. Eli and Diana, siblings by blood, take a bold and last-minute trip in an attempt to escape from their lives, but fate may find that they discover themselves instead. Read along as Eli introspectively reflects on a journey of family, love, and soul.

The reader may find themselves angry and emotionally unstable at times, but embracing those feelings and accepting them as their own is what this novel really asks us all to do- to find ourselves within Eli Greene and to accept life as it truly is.